A JAN KOKK MYSTERY

WHO KILLED VAN GOGH?

ROY F. SULLIVAN

authorHOUSE®

AuthorHouse™
1663 Liberty Drive
Bloomington, IN 47403
www.authorhouse.com
Phone: 1 (800) 839-8640

Published by AuthorHouse   02/09/2016

ISBN: 978-1-5049-7858-3 (sc)
ISBN: 978-1-5049-7857-6 (e)

Print information available on the last page.

This book is printed on acid-free paper.

TABLE OF CONTENTS

ILLUSTRATIONS BY THE AUTHOR

DEDICATED TO NANCY: AGENT, EDITOR,
PHOTOGRAPHER, REVIEWER, AND CRITIC

This work is fiction, pure fiction. All references to people, places, businesses and organizations are used fictionally. Names, titles, locations, characters, lyrics, and incidents are the product of the author's imagination. Any resemblance to actuality is the result of chance, not intent.

OTHER BOOKS BY THE AUTHOR

(ROY F SULLIVAN or RF SULLIVAN)

"Scattered Graves: The Civil War Campaigns of Confederate Brigadier General and Cherokee Chief Stand Watie"

"The Civil War in Texas and the Southwest"

"The Texas Revolution: The Texas Navies"

"The Texas Revolution: Tejano Heroes"

"Escape from Phnom Penh: Americans in the Cambodian War"

"Escape from the Pentagon"

"Reflections on Command: Kit Carson at the First Battle of Adobe Walls"

"A Jan Kokk Mystery: The Curacao Connection"

"A Jan Kokk Mystery: Murder Cruises the Antilles"

"A Jan Kokk Mystery: Gambol in Vegas"

"A Jan Kokk Mystery: Crises in Kerrville"

AUTHOR'S NOTE: The Marechaussee mentioned herein is the Royal Dutch Gendarmerie, one of the four military services of the armed forces of the Netherlands. The missions of the Marechaussee include combating international crime and illegal immigration, guarding the national borders, assisting the Dutch Police, securing airports, riot control and protection plus performing as military police of the Dutch armed forces. If these functions were not enough, the Marechaussee also protects the royal castles and the residence of the Dutch Prime Minister. The Marechaussee, numbering about 600 personnel, is commanded by a lieutenant general responsible to the Minister of Defense of the Netherlands.

ONE

AMSTERDAM

Like a stripper the sun alternately peeked through mouse-colored clouds--then hid--over an awakening Amsterdam. Swirls and dense mist from the North Sea defied hardy Dutch folk struggling to get to work on time in their big city.

"*Verdomme!*" She swore at the passing cyclist who sloshed her short black skirt with cold water as she locked her bicycle into one of Amsterdam's thousands of cycle racks. The communal rack she used was on Kalverstraat, just a half block from her job at a prestigious old-quarter art gallery.

Wet but unbowed, the blue-eyed, blonde, obviously Dutch twenty-year old strode toward the gallery's towering gray stone façade with its simple polished brass plate announcing GALERIE GOGEN.

"If your appearance is understated, your prices certainly make up for it." She usually quipped aloud as she entered her workplace.

But not today.

She was late for work again. By the time she took off aqua tennies and replaced them with the black high heels expected in one of the old town's most famous art galleries, it was be ten minutes past the hour.

Her employer, Karl Gogen, antiquities and art dealer, would be smirking at her beside the front door of the gallery unless he was cajoling an early arriving customer. Often a passing tourist distracted *Meneer* (Mr.) Gogen, middle-aged, bald and resplendent in black suit, dazzling white shirt, gold links and cream tie.

Susse hoped today was such a day. If she escaped her boss's front door scrutiny, there was still his usual grasping for her arm or hand to be avoided.

Inside the gallery entrance no one was in sight so she scooted into the small enclosure marked "Staff Only" hiding the office coffee percolator.

Hurriedly she filled the empty pot with water, measured and scooped-in coffee, then turned on the switch. She hung her wet beret and raincoat from the hat tree and entered the ladies lounge.

Brushing furiously at the damp ends of her page boy hair, she assessed the damage done by the careless cyclist, male of course. Unblinking eyes stared back at her pixie face. As she applied gloss the door to the ladies' room banged open.

"Late again, Susse?" Margue Stassel, the gallery secretary, croaked. "You'd better be extra nice to boss Gogen today. If you want to be employed here tomorrow."

Stassel giggled. "At least you'd better let him pinch a feel without telling that wife of his."

Still smirking Stassel stood beside Susse at the big rectangular mirror, patting her graying coiffure. The two were comrades-in-arms, both coping with a boss who thought his winks and advances were an unwritten part of their contracts.

"Did he ever reward you with chocolates or flowers for favors?" asked Susse. She grimaced, imagining Margue and Gogen entangled on the stock room's receiving table.

Margue shook her head emphatically. "Not me. The salary here is good, but not that good. How do you keep him at bay?"

Susse brushed the front of her silk blouse with a hand. "He knows that I know and regularly talk to his wife--is how.

"If he touched me, I'd tell her in a Dutch second. She'd scratch him up, then call the police and charge him.

"It works so far." Susse paused pensively before heading back to the percolator.

Leaning toward the mirror, Margue frowned at her sagging bust line. "You know he's off to Brussels this afternoon? 'Buying trip', he calls it. Probably going to find some girl--*belle de jour*--they call it? And spend the night," she added with a wink.

"Must be nice to afford luxury." Hearing the door chime announcing a customer, Susse quickly moved toward the front door. Maybe a sale this early in the day would allay Gogen's unwanted attention.

She whispered to herself. "So his wife will be solo and lonely tonight. Wonder how soon Sophie will call me with an invitation?"

Susse spend an hour with the first customer, reviewing catalogues detailing Rembrandt and van Gogh reproductions. Gogen, the boss and gallery owner, breezed by her table as she explained the estimated value of the actual paintings, some of which were exhibited in the Rembrandt Museum just two blocks away.

She handed the customer, a visiting portly German from Stuttgart, a cup of coffee as she led him down the corridor hung with large framed reproductions of famous painters' works. She also walked him through displays of modern Dutch painters: the DeKaus, the Finkerns and van Hohers. Appreciative oohs and ahhs from the German marked their passage through the next corridor, raising her hopes of a sale.

On a whim, she led him through the first hall again.

Susse thought the man was certain to place an order for one of the reproductions. Instead he asked her to have lunch with him. Raised eyebrows hinted at dinner and dancing--who knows what--that evening.

Smiling, she declined saying she hoped she'd see him in the gallery again tomorrow. The German made a face and left, leaving the front door ajar.

"No sale?" Walking up behind her, Gogen blinked through thick oval glasses. "Perhaps you should have been more receptive."

Smiling broadly, he stopped in front of Susse. "How about lunch with me at my club? We need to discuss next week's anniversary sale which I'm depending on you to organize."

"I've brought my lunch today, *Meneer* Gogen," she said politely. "But thank you very much for the invitation."

He lifted his hands, turning to his office in the rear. "Ah, well," he opened the door.

"Perhaps next time?" With that he disappeared inside his office.

A second later, he reappeared. "Next time, please call me Karl."

At three that afternoon, Susse sat at her desk filling on-line orders from overseas customers. Margue filed her nails while discussing the weather and weekend plans.

Suddenly Margue cleared her throat.

Recognizing the other's usual signal for a question, Susse laid down her pen. "Yes?"

"Any new boyfriends, Susse?"

"Did you say new ones or good ones?"

"I wish you'd introduce me to either kind," Margue leaned forward. "Let's go to a coffeehouse this afternoon and celebrate the boss's absence with drinks and supper. Wouldn't it be wonderful if he missed the return flight tomorrow?"

Susse replaced the reading glasses she'd just removed. "That's as unlikely as our meeting someone interesting in one of those places crowded with teenagers, tourists and *ganja* smoke."

She winked at her friend. "I'm waiting and looking for that perfect man, Marg."

Margue refilled their cups. "Then you'd better have more coffee, dear. You're in for a long, long wait."

Suddenly Gogen emerged from his office, briefcase in hand. Margue dropped the nail file and pretended to answer the telephone.

"Gogen Gallery," she said brightly, fooling no one.

"Good afternoon, ladies," Gogen frowned at Margue. "I'm off to the airport. Can I trust you two to lock-up at the close of business?"

Both women quickly responded. "Yes, *Menheer.*"

As the front door closed after their boss, Margue turned to Susse. "Shall we close the place *one* hour early or right now?"

"We'd better wait until his flight has gone. He might come back to check on us if it's postponed or cancelled."

"*Got verhoede,* God forbid." Margue fretted, reaching for her handbag as the telephone on Susse's desk rang twice.

TWO

Susse pressed the door buzzer at Number 8, Heigerstraat promptly at six, having returned to her apartment for a shower and change of the black work ensemble. Tonight she chose a pair of faded and fashionably knee-less jeans, a woolen North Sea sweater and moccasins.

Immediately the door opened, revealing a stern-looking Sophie, Karl's wife. She wore a too-large business suit, white shirt and tie. No smile.

About to giggle, Susse studied the other's attire, obviously borrowed from the absent husband. Then she stepped forward, arms outstretched in greeting.

Sophie sidestepped her and extended a finger toward her husband's at-home office. "This way to my office, Miss," Sophie directed in clipped tones.

Susse blinked at the unexpected business suit and formal greeting but followed Sophie into the small office. Sophie stood behind a large walnut desk, festooned with iPads and mobile phones.

Shooting a small hand across the massive desk, straight-faced Sophie introduced herself. "*Menheer* Gogen.

"And you, Miss…?"

"How do you do, Mr. Gogen. My name is Susse."

"Please have a seat, Miss Susse." Sophie motioned at a straight chair placed immediately in front of the desk.

Suppressing a grin, Susse understood. Sophie was creating another game, this one parodying the husband probably cavorting in Brussels by now.

At their last game, Susse played the part of a male doctor and Sophie, a nervous teenaged patient. Susse wore a white coat, a pair of Karl's absurd glasses, and flourished a length of black licorice for a stethoscope. She held the "stethoscope" against Sophie's breast.

Susse frowned. "A bit irregular, young lady. Has something or someone excited you?"

That was last week's game. This was a new one.

Sophie, playing her husband, peeked over the oval glasses. "Your full name, Miss?"

As she spoke, Sophie slid an application form to the center of the massive desk.

"Susse Thankker, sir."

"Very good, Miss Thankker." Sophie slowly wrote the name on the form. "Address?"

Straight-faced, Susse stammered. "One twenty Backner Lane, sir."

"Backner. Backnner." Looking up, Sophie paused. "One n or two?"

"One n, Mr. Gogen."

"Ah," Sophie looked up. "You remember my name."

"Of course. You are a well-known art dealer and business leader in Amsterdam, sir."

Sophie beamed. "How wise of you to have researched my establishment before applying for a position at the famous Galerie Gogen. Splendid, splendid. I commend you.

"I presume you saw my advertisement for these positions in *De Telegraaff*?"

"Yes, Mr. Gogen."

"Now."

Sophie glanced over the oval rims. "Are you applying for the research assistant position or the position as my personal and private secretary?"

"The latter, Mr. Gogen."

"And what are your qualifications for this sensitive and very private position, Miss? You understand that my many cut-throat competitors will attempt to obtain private information about Galerie Gogen by any and all means, lawful or otherwise?"

Wide-eyed, Susse nodded. "I completely understand, sir."

"Those thieves would like nothing better than to know my personal schedules, names of my associates and customers. They'd pay you highly for such tidbits."

Susse looked penitent. "I certainly would not participate in such activities, Mr. Gogen. You can depend on me."

"Are you *certain* I can depend on your discretion?" Sophie tossed the glasses aside.

"Certainly, sir. I'll be like that Egyptian sphinx."

"Come over here, young lady," Sophie indicated the chair next to her own. "I want you to carefully study these work standards expected of my private and personal secretary."

"Yes, Mr. Gogen."

"Closer, closer," Sophie urged.

"What is that delightful fragrance you're wearing?"

"It's French, Mr. Gogen. Called *Adore.*"

"Perhaps we should seal your understanding of the many and varied duties of the private and personal position you seem to desire?"

With that, Sophie deftly lifted an icy, beaded bottle from a bucket beneath the desk. She adroitly poured two flutes of champagne.

"To your new job, charming Miss Susse!"

"To my new job, Mr. Gogen!"

With that they toasted and drained the flutes. Susse held out hers for more. Sophie refilled both.

Again they emptied their glasses, then threw them into the fireplace. They enthusiastically kissed to the sounds of shattered crystal.

THREE

She nudged Sophie snuggled against her in the big king-size bed. "I hear something downstairs!"

"Um, um," Sophie murmured, then stirred. "What time is it?"

"Sophie!"

Suddenly alert, Susse trembled as she shook Sophie. "I think someone's coming up the stairs!"

"What? It can't be Karl! He's not supposed to return until tomorrow."

Susse reached for the nightlight on her side.

Sophie hissed. "Don't turn on that light."

"Who else could it be if not Karl returning early?"

"Oh, my God! Why would he be back so soon? Trying to trap us?"

Susse scrambled out from under the coverlet as the door opened. A silhouette appeared, framed in the doorway by the hall light.

Husband Karl stood there, without glasses, peering into the darkened room.

"What, what?" Puzzled, he saw the mix of clothing scattered on the floor. He recognized one of his business suits, shirt and tie amid the jumble.

Then he saw Susse, trembling beside--his side--the big bed. He lunged forward, grabbing her by the hair.

Dragging Susse across the floor, he knocked over the bedside lamp, radio and clock.

Sophie screamed. "Help! Police!"

Karl glared at Susse, scrambling to her feet. "You! In my bed!"

"And Sophie!" Trembling with rage, he pointed. "My wife!"

He stared at them, the shock of finding his wife in bed with another momentarily stifled thought.

He wrenched Susse by her hair again and she crumpled to the floor.

Sophie, transfixed, sat upright, screaming abruptly stopped.

She commanded Karl in an angry tone. "Let her go! Get out of here!"

He released Susse and stood there, dumbly obeying.

"I can't believe this!" Partially recovering, he shouted at them, then picked the clock off the floor and threw it at Sophie.

Yelling, he kicked Susse's clothing towards her. "Get out of my bed! Get out of my house!"

"Get out!" He backhanded her as she stooped to retrieve her jeans. Wide-eyed with fright, she scooped up sweater and panties and ran.

As Susse disappeared, Karl moved toward Sophie. He began striking her face, arms, shoulders, wherever and as hard as he could.

His attack aroused Sophie's own fury. "Stop it, Karl! I'll call the police and have you arrested and jailed!

"You'll pay dearly for every slap! You'll be in all the papers! You'll be ruined! I'll make sure of that!"

He turned and left, slamming the door so hard their silver-framed wedding picture fell to the floor, broken. Cursing, he descended the stairs, chasing Susse.

Opening the front door he looked out at her already in the street. Still putting on the moccasins, Susse stumbled, then ran toward the tram station.

"Never come here again, you slut! You're fired!

"Never come back to this house or the gallery! I'll send your belongings or give them to the Red Cross!

"I hope you starve to death, whoring in the red light district, *De Wallen*!"

FOUR

THE HAGUE

"Never been treated so well," I blew a kiss at the vivacious airlines hostess refilling my cocktail glass. I admired Lillian's undulating progress up the aisle on the short KLM flight from Amsterdam to The Hague, the Dutch capital.

I motioned her back with a question. "Have time for a drink in the airport lounge before you return to that cold lonely apartment?"

Lillian bent over slightly to look six foot four, curling gray-hair, tanned Jan Kokk in the eye. She tugged at the loose seat belt. "Need to buckle up, Mr. Kokk. We're landing soon.

"Or may I do it for you?"

Without waiting, she clicked my belt and drew it tight. "You don't have time for a drink at the airport, Mr. Kokk. I just read the captain's message about you."

I gasped, quickly loosening the constricting strap.

Short of breath, "What message?" was all I could muster.

"You're being taken off the plane ahead of our first class passengers to a special room where your luggage and a driver await to carry you off someplace."

She eyed me. "You get to miss the customs check!"

Lillian bent down lower. "What did you do, Mr. Kokk? Threaten the Queen?"

I blinked at her news but persisted. "How about a rain check on that drink, followed by dinner at the hotel?"

"Only if the Queen can spare you, Mr. Kokk." Lillian flounced up the aisle to her folding seat in the front of the airbus. On her way she palmed her card and cell phone number into my hand.

Just as described, on landing I was motioned to the front of the aircraft, past inquiring looks from the first-class passengers, and down a corridor to a private room. A beaming uniformed Dutch officer wearing the gold six-pointed insignia of a major greeted me at the door.

"Mr. Kokk? Mr. Jan Kokk? Welcome. I'm Major Erik Loftner." He saluted and reached for the bulging leather valise I carried.

"That's my cognac," I demurred. "You can't have it, *Majoor.*"

"Sorry, sir. Perhaps you prefer I address you by your former rank, *Eerste-Luitenant?*"

Shaking my head in disbelief, I looked about the smart, oak-paneled room. Where were the others of my old unit? I'd flown from Curacao for a rowdy reunion with the Marechaussee comrades with whom I had served in Surinam.

"Where are my old chums, Major? I expected to see a dozen gray-haired, capricious men of my advanced age. Surely they're not all dead?"

Loftner retrieved my suitcase and headed for the exit. "If you'll follow me, *Menheer* Kokk, I'll explain.

"We're off to your hotel, the *Ibis Den Haag* in the city center. There you'll see the others of your platoon gathered for the reunion.

"I'll also brief you about a ceremony arranged for you tomorrow at the Defense Ministry."

Mystified, I followed the officer to curbside where an official blue and white sedan waited.

"We just established a new Guinness record for exiting an aircraft at Schiphol, getting through customs and finding a taxi! You're a wonder Major."

The driver shoved my suitcase into the trunk and the major and I climbed into the back seat.

"You mentioned a ceremony? I'm afraid you picked up the wrong person from my flight.

"I'm plain Jan Kokk from Curacao. True, I was wounded in Surinam and medically discharged from the Marechaussee. Nothing I did in Surinam merits a ceremony.

"To avoid embarrassment I suggest I get out here with my suitcase and you return to find the correct person you were detailed to pick up. After all, my name is a common one."

"You're very modest, Mr. Kokk. You are that important person. I'm honored to be your escort while you're at The Hague.

"If I may continue, sir. Here is your schedule for the reunion events, beginning with cocktails in the hotel main dining room. That begins at 1900 hours this evening. Uniform is casual. I will be there to assist you of course."

I couldn't believe it. "Assist me?"

Unfazed, Major Loftner continued. "Dinner in that same dining room begins at 2030 hours with the customary call to order and toast to the Queen. Your seat is at the head table and I will guide you to it."

"I think I can handle cocktails and dinner by myself, Major. What's this ceremony you mentioned?"

Without a blink, Loftner continued. "I'll join you for breakfast at 0900 hours tomorrow morning in the same dining room. After breakfast, we will drive to the ministry where the ceremony takes place."

"Wait, wait!" I laughed so hard my eyes watered. "You see, I never told a major 'to wait' while I was on active duty.

"I'm really puzzled about this ceremony tomorrow morning."

Loftner passed me a blue and white folder. "Mr. Kokk--*Eerste-Luitenant* Kokk--you are to be decorated for valor while engaging an armed enemy in Surinam.

"That day, 12 October, you were seriously wounded. Despite those wounds, you refused medical evacuation and continued to lead your platoon against a larger enemy force repeatedly attacking your position.

"You personally carried two of your wounded to safety and you continued to hold that surrounded position until later relieved by an entire company of the Marechaussee.

"You may well ask why has recognition of your bravery taken so long? It is because the majority of your platoon was also wounded that day. They were medically evacuated before they could relate what you did. I apologize but it has taken years to reconstruct the details of that day's actions--your bravery--from the survivors.

"You yourself were seriously wounded and evacuated to the military hospital in Utrecht."

As the sedan stopped in front of a large hotel, I frowned. "Major Loftner, I tell you plainly. I was neither heroic nor brave.

"I was simply trying to keep the enemy out of our position and get my wounded to safety. I cannot accept an award. Please tell your ministry--or whoever--it has the wrong man. I was no hero.

"Sorry to place you in this predicament," I told the baffled officer. "No hero," I repeated.

"You'll have to inform the ministry and cancel or change the ceremony for the proper person. Not me."

Loftner leaped from the parked sedan, turned and saluted me. "Like it or not, Mr. Kokk. You were a brave leader and hero. Your men all confirmed it."

Major Loftner thumbed through another folder as I got out of the car. "You are Jan Kokk, forty-nine years of age, born in Willemstad, Curacao?

"You are six foot four inches in height and weigh 230 pounds? Have gray hair and moustache? This is your personnel file and your photograph?"

He held an opened personnel record in front of me.

I returned his salute with a sigh then followed Loftner and the driver into the hotel's garish entrance hall.

"I repeat," I persisted at the reception desk while registering and taking a room key.

"No hero, no ceremony. I hope you can clear this up before our next formation at cocktails and dinner this evening. Thank you."

I turned and headed for the elevator.

FIVE

AMSTERDAM

She grabbed the telephone, knowing who rang her number twice, hung up, then called twice again. It had been their private signal for the past year.

"Sophie, are you all right? Are you hurt badly?"

Tearing, Susse wiped her eyes before speaking again. "I feel terrible, running out on you, leaving you with that crazy, vicious man!"

"Don't cry, kitten," Sophie soothed. "Just listen carefully because I don't have much time before Karl returns."

"Are you okay? Are you home?"

"I'm fine except for a few bruises and a black eye, which I've had photographed for evidence. No, I'm not home.

"I'm at a street pay phone. Karl has all our house phones monitored. Now listen. Did you receive your belongings from the gallery?"

"Yes. And something else I must ask you about."

"I know, I know, love. I told Karl he had to write you a glowing letter of reference for a better position somewhere. I threatened to call the police to come to the house with sirens blazing and the press following. I'd show them my black eye and bruises and tell them exactly how he attacked us."

Sophie's tone softened "Are you all right? Did he hurt you badly knocking you down?"

Susse ignored the question. "How can we stay in touch? I miss you already."

"Just as I miss you, dear. I've been thinking. Karl is so jealous and alert. I'll send you a short message in the personal section of the *Telegraaff*. Look for messages for Alexis. That's you."

"Where can we meet that's safe?"

"I picked out a little place on Leidseplein called *De Oesterbar*. Know it?"

14

"Sure. Why it?"

"Karl hates oysters," Sophie giggled. "We'll always meet there at two in the afternoon. Okay?"

"Got it. Be very careful, Sophie. He's a madman!"

"Don't I know! Must go now. Love you!"

The call ended with a click before she could reply. Susse reached for another tissue and wiped her eyes. Absently, she picked up Karl's letter of recommendation contained in the box of personal items delivered to her apartment.

Knowing how her ex-boss hated her, Susse reread portions of the glowing letter of recommendation from him. Frowning, she realized how insistently Sophie must have wheedled. What price had Karl extracted from Sophie for this wonderful letter of recommendation?

Miss Thankker is highly knowledgeable in art, its history, artifacts and paintings, particularly in regard to the works of the Dutch masters.

She is poised and gracious with the many art critics and customers daily visiting the famous showrooms of Galerie Gogen. Many favorable comments have been received about her knowledge, abilities and assistance.

Without hesitation I highly recommend Miss Thankker for any responsible position in any art museum or gallery.

(signed) KARL GOGEN
Director, Galerie Gogen.

She stared at his signature, despising him and his treatment. Again she wondered. What had this letter cost Sophie in pain and humiliation?

Gritting her teeth, Susse waved the recommendation triumphantly.

"Tomorrow morning, I'll get the morning paper and start looking for a new job!"

SIX

THE HAGUE

Dapper in coat and tie, I marched into the first floor cocktail lounge, hoping my old companions were gathering there.

Immediately a half dozen men I hadn't seen for years surrounded me. Handshaking, backslapping and a frenzy of welcoming voices drowned out the music coming from a quartet playing in a far corner of the lounge.

Soon the musical quartet surrendered, retreating to a farther section of the big room. As they withdrew, one of my former platoon took over the vacated piano and began playing soldier melodies.

I motioned to the beaming female bartender for a round of drinks.

"Not on my watch, Lieutenant!" Former Corporal Heiter stood shakily atop a barstool, shouting. "This round's on me!"

More cheers erupted as new drinks were passed around. I helped myself to one of the steins of beer offered from a tray. I motioned to the bartender, leaning forward to speak to her over the hubbub.

"Next one's on me, lovely lady. If you need help back there," I nodded at her side of the big oak bar. "I'm ready, steady and loose."

She puckered her lips. "What kind of help are you offering, handsome big man?"

I whispered in her ear. She guffawed at my answer.

The soldier piano player beckoned me to join the chorus of a favorite drinking song. Relieving the bartender of a tray of filled glasses, I slowly worked my way through the crowd at the piano.

Someone shouted. "Sing, Lieutenant! Sing!"

Soon the bartender, delivering another tray of steins, tugged at my elbow. "Thought I might as well join you. Can't let you have all the fun!"

Whooping, I hoisted her to the top of the piano where she sat, passing out more beer to ecstatic singers.

Stepping behind the piano, I tapped the shoulder of one of the singers, formerly the platoon sergeant.

"Your singing hasn't improved since Surinam, Sergeant Schreiner."

"Not has your waistline, Lieutenant!"

We pounded each other on the back before I lowered my voice. "Wonder if you'd do me a huge favor."

Schreiner wiped the foam from his lips. "You know I'd march through a cobra patch in the dark for you, sir."

"I need a list of our missing men. I mean those KIA and WIA during that last action. I intend to read their names at a ceremony we may have to attend tomorrow morning. As our platoon sergeant, I bet you a case of Amstel beer that you remember all their names and how they became casualties."

"Can do easy, Lieutenant. I'll still be happy with the case of Amstel."

"I'm indebted to you. Think you can handle it tonight?"

"Consider it done, sir." Schneider jerked his head toward the door. "Looks like that young major over there is trying to get your attention."

I pumped his hand again. "Thanks. See you in the dining room." Turning, I blew a kiss at our happy female bartender still seated on top of the piano.

Major Loftner, resplendent in dress blue uniform, saluted as I approached, causing a stir along the old soldiers standing at the bar.

"Sorry to interrupt, sir. The brigade commander, Colonel Rosent, invites you to join him for a drink in the lobby.

"Is this about that ceremony?"

"Yes sir."

"Good. I have something to tell the good colonel."

SEVEN

After the formal dinner, I excused myself from Colonel Rosent's table and joined my comrades.

Corporal Smitten was the first to welcome me. "Enough chow, Lieutenant?"

"Call me Jan," I protested to the delight of the others.

"Who's still able to remember the words to our old marching song?" I asked.

Smitten rose from his chair and began singing in a bass voice before the rest of us joined him.

When the war is over, we will all enlist again,
When the war is over, we will all enlist again,
Ja, Ja, when the war is over, we will all enlist again,
We will, LIKE HELL we will!

Brandishing an empty stein, I joined in the chorus. Smitten pointed to the grins and smiles of the occupants of the head table and nudged me.

Holding up a hand, I suggested. "Let's go back to the bar and see if that blonde bartender still loves us."

"On the way! On the way!'

Like a textbook platoon leader, I stood and waved. "Follow me!"

A little wobbly but upright, former Platoon Sergeant Schreiner--not to be outdone--jumped to his feet.

"Fall in!" he commanded.

Everyone immediately reacted by forming at the side of the table as if they were still soldiers.

"Right face! Forward march!" They obeyed just as they had in the past, marching from the main dining room to the applause of the other diners.

Major Loftner edged up to me in the lounge bar as I whispered new propositions to the beaming bartender.

He stammered. "Mr. Kokk, er, Lieutenant Kokk…"

Tiring of formality, I said "Call me Jan. What may I do for you, Major?"

"Sir, I need to know what you and the colonel decided about tomorrow's ceremony. He didn't tell me anything before he departed."

"Well," I began as my favorite bartender passed Loftner a stein. "We decided that the ceremony is a go, with the proviso that I accept this award--whatever it is--in the name of each member of my platoon who was there that day.

"I made it clear to the colonel that I am reading the name of each man of my platoon, including the casualties. The award is for *all* of us.

"By the way. What is the award?"

Loftner wiped his lips. "It's the Order of the Bronze Lion, the *Bronzen Loeuw.*"

I whistled. It was a high decoration. "That ought to please the men. Especially when I get the Commandant's approval to have the medal and a plaque listing their names mounted in the Marechaussee chapel."

Shaking his head, Loftner finished his beer. "I'm amazed, sir, how easily you get such changes approved by not only our colonel, but our three-star commandant as well.

"You should have been a diplomat! You'd have made The Hague the capital of Europe by now!

Uncomfortable with his words, I grimaced. "Are you and I still meeting for breakfast at 0900?"

"Yes sir. I'm sure you'll be highly presentable for the ceremony"

"My troops and I *all* will be highly presentable. Good night, Major."

"Good night, sir."

I turned back to my comrades loudly singing another stanza.

Captain had a bottle and he gave us all a drink,
Captain had a bottle and he gave us all a drink,
Captain had a bottle and he gave us all a drink,
He did, LIKE HELL HE DID!

Trudi, the bartender, motioned and reserved me a vacant stool at the bar.

"How smart are you, Jan?"

"Just barely, lovely lady. Why?"

"I'm wondering how you'll get all these loud rascals to leave within the next ten minutes."

Eyebrows raised, I waited for her punch line.

"I can't close the bar and take you home with me until they're all gone."

EIGHT

At eleven the next morning, the sun glinted brightly as I stood at attention beside my platoon in the middle of the Marechaussee parade field.

Even ex-Platoon Sergeant Schreiner admitted the platoon looked very good in just-issued kepi hats of Marechausee blue and white. When told we'd be facing the sun while in ceremonial formation, I requested the men be issued visored hats.

Major Loftner shrugged, thinking my late request would be turned down. Luckily, the commandant seemed pleased to provide the headgear.

Also requested at the last minute, a military band from the royal household briskly paraded and performed to our front.

At a dais in front of our small formation, the adjutant motioned for the band to stop playing.

He stepped to a microphone and began reading the citation accompanying the decoration being awarded in the name of the Queen.

"By direction of Her Majesty the Queen, the military Order of the Bronze Lion is awarded to Marechaussee *Eerste-Luitenant* Jan Kokk and platoon for valor in connection with military operations against a hostile armed force in Surinam…"

I hoped the lengthy citation would end soon. All of us in formation suffered from the ravages of heat, lack of sleep and too much Amstel.

I had managed to return to the hotel at 0700, just in time to shower, change into my only suit and meet Major Loftner downstairs.

"What was I thinking?" I argued with myself on the way to breakfast. "I'm no longer a young man capable of all-nighters."

On the parade ground, the adjutant stopped reading the citation and called my rank and name.

"Front and center."

Trying not to limp, I stepped forward to face the commandant who wore a dazzling white dress uniform replete with decorations.

This was the easy part. The commandant pinned the decoration on me, smiled and shook my hand.

Now it was my turn to salute, then stand beside the commandant and colonel on the dais.

Holding the list of names prepared by Schreiner last night, I began slowly reading.

"It is my privilege, Commandant, to accept this decoration in the name of the soldiers of the Second Platoon, 33rd Marechaussee Company, whom you see before you. Not all the members of the Platoon are present since the casualties resulting from the engagement of 12 October 1981 accounted for forty percent of our effective strength.

"The number of the enemy attacking our position was estimated to be four times our own. The men of the Second Platoon held our position for over twenty-four hours until relieved by an entire company.

"I now read the names of all members of the Second Platoon including our departed comrades. Their collective valor was responsible for the successful, sustained defense of our position.

"The followed Mareschaussee were killed in action: Sergeant Erst van Hooser, Corporal Gerd Ridenhour, Corporal Hans Heffner, Private First Class Henri Blattner, Private First Class Andre Shribner...."

I read the names of the killed and wounded, then the names of the survivors. Saluting the commandant, I returned to my position with the platoon.

The band marched by, escorting a standard bearer holding aloft the coat of arms of the Royal Netherlands Marechaussee.

Stepping in front of the platoon, Schreiner led a series of hurrahs, then called the platoon to attention and marched it from the field, following the band.

Remaining behind, I thanked the commandant and colonel and saluted as they departed.

"Time for a cold Amstel," I said it aloud, wondering if my haste was caused by the thought of an Amstel or Trudi the bartender. Before reaching the sedan to return to the hotel, Major Loftner intercepted me with a quizzical look.

"How'd it go, Major?"

"Couldn't have been better, sir. Perfect! Congratulations, Jan." He handed me a stiff white envelope.

"What's this?"

Loftner chuckled. "I think it's your next assignment. Good luck with it!"

NINE

AMSTERDAM

Her telephone rang twice. Susse immediately picked it up. No tone. Hastily she replaced it before it rang twice more.

"Sophie?"

"Yes, Susse."

"You're very punctual." She eyed her kitchen clock. "Are you alright?"

"Sure. Glad you saw that little ad for Alexis I put in yesterday's paper."

"Worked like a charm, Sophie. Tell me, how you're really feeling? Is that maniac husband still abusing you? Why don't you report him to the police? Better yet, leave him!"

"Then I lose what leverage over Karl that I have at the moment. That's what got that dandy letter of recommendation. Is it doing you any good??"

"Bless you, Sophie. Without it, I'd be forever looking for a job."

"Does that mean you have a job already?"

"It does! Guess where?"

"Tell me!"

"At the van Gogh Museum on Potterstraat!"

"Wow! Congratulations! Wish I were with you right now to celebrate! What's the job?"

"Well, I'm just the clerk of the moment. You know, make the office coffee, put paper in the duplicator, run errands for the director.

"'Docent' is the official title, but the director seems to like me. I think eventually I'll get a better job and a raise."

Susse's tone deepened. "When do I get to see you?"

"Be patient. It's too soon. Karl watches me like a tamer in the lion cage. I'm happy you're doing so well. Bruises all gone?"

"Yeah, I'm fine but lonely."

"Hang on, Susse. I miss you, too. Terribly."

Sophie paused. "I want to see you so badly. Is there something wrong with the two of us?"

Strident, Susse almost shouted. "Not at all! As long as there're men like Karl, there'll be women like us."

"Got to go. Keep an eye on those personals, Alexis."

That same morning at The Hague, I pushed away from the hearty breakfast Trudi had prepared us in her tiny kitchen.

"Delicious! You're incredible! And your coffee?" I smacked my lips while enjoying a second cup.

"Superb!"

"That mean you won't leave me for a younger woman?" Trudi teased.

"Of course, I would," I teased back. "But I'd feel very badly about it!"

Her shoe hit the door as I closed it on my way out. With a wave of the hand, I hailed a cab to take me back to the hotel.

Today's reunion schedule called for a bus ride through the royal gardens followed by lunch at the Ministry of Defense.

Habit made me check my father's big gold pocket watch. There was also an early afternoon appointment with the chaplain at the Marechaussee chapel about where the *Bronzen Loeuw* decoration and silver plaque were to be displayed.

The plaque was in a shop being engraved with the names of the casualties from our last action as well as all surviving platoon members.

With a start, I felt the hard edge of the envelope handed me yesterday by Major Loftner. In my haste to see Trudi, I'd forgotten it.

After giving the taxi driver my destination, I slid open the heavy white envelope. It contained an engraved invitation to "confer" with a deputy minister after today's reunion luncheon. The purpose of the meeting wasn't mentioned, heightening my curiosity.

TEN

Usually placid, I may have frowned, sitting in the chair before the desk of the Dutch Deputy Minister of Arts and Culture. I presumed the invitation to meet with "a deputy minister" was from the Defense Ministry, not Arts and Culture.

"Thank you for coming, Mr. Kokk," the short, stout deputy minister wearing an obvious toupee leaned over his massive desk, offering a cigar humidor.

"I understand your confusion at being here instead of at Defense. At my request a colleague generously seconded you and your valuable services to us in A&C.

"My ministry has an unusual, historical case to offer you in your role as a private investigator, not as a former military officer.

"I call the case 'unusual'. More accurately I could describe it as being highly significant to Dutch art, thus to that of the entire world."

Thoughts tumbling, I selected a slim Macanudo cigar from the humidor. "My surprise must be evident, Mr. Minister. My work is seldom publicized and is little known in Curacao, much less here in the Netherlands."

All the time studying my host, I picked matches from my vest and lighted the Macanudo.

The deputy minister scrutinized me as I puffed his fine cigar.

"That's untrue, Mr. Kokk," he shook his head. "Our national police follow your many successes. One may become a case study in their academy's curriculum.

"An example with which even I'm familiar is your case of that Antilles cargo freighter from which the crew--one by one--mysteriously disappeared at sea."

(Author's Note: "Murder Cruises the Antilles")

The deputy looked expectantly at me. "You and the female security officer ended up being the only survivors to face the murderer."

"You flatter me, Minister," I acknowledged. "Your cigar is good as your memory."

I leaned forward. "What may I do for your ministry?"

The deputy cradled the ash of his cigar before sliding a folder across the desk. "We would like you to investigate the death, suicide, murder--whatever--of one of our most famous countrymen."

"Who?"

"Vincent van Gogh, the painter."

I probably blanched. "Minister, I'm particularly ignorant about van Gogh or any Dutch painter. Knowing nothing about that subject, you could safely say that I'm the least qualified investigator in the world for such an assignment."

I considered standing up to leave. "I'm afraid, Minister, that someone has misled you about the plain, simple man sitting before you, Jan Kokk from Curacao."

I touched my forehead. "Are you serious about investigating a death that occurred…."

No mathematician, I closed my eyes for a moment. "What…? Over a hundred years ago?"

He chuckled. "One hundred twenty-six years ago to be precise, Mr. Kokk."

"Minister, someone's been watching too much *Cold Case* on American TV.

"Why…evidence is like the fog. None remains after a little sunshine. One hundred twenty-six years provides plenty of sunshine."

"Mr. Kokk, you wouldn't be here if we lacked confidence in you and your methods. We are certain you have the experience and ability to answer this ancient mystery.

"So confident," he motioned at the folder, "that we're offering you a lucrative, all expenses, open-end contract."

He began pacing behind the desk, waving me back to my chair.

"Who killed or murdered Vincent van Gogh? Was his death a suicide as popularly believed?

"It is in our national interest to know the truth about the great Dutch artist's death. His reputation has long been sullied by rumors of suicide. It's past time the truth about his untimely and early death is known. Our Dutch psyche demands the truth.

"Bear with me, Mr. Kokk, while I mention other aspects of your government's generous offer.

"Within the folder is the original French police report, such as it is, about this tragedy. Our own police investigation conducted a week after van Gogh's death is also there.

"We have assurances from the French government that its police, especially the Surete, will cooperate fully with you. We have hired an art expert to instruct you, prior to your departure for France, about van Gogh and his last works. That should give you some idea of the man's character and state of mind prior to his death.

"That expert also speaks French fluently and will act as your translator and assistant. Hotel reservations are awaiting you in Amsterdam, where you will meet the Director of the van Gogh Museum where the expert is employed. Any briefings you desire will be arranged by the expert, your assistant.

"First class air tickets have been purchased for you and your assistant. An auto has been leased for your use in France. In short, your government has gone to great lengths--including a substantial salary--to induce you to take this awesome assignment.

"I assure you, Mr. Kokk. Your other successes will pale in comparison with this one. You will be changing art history, not only for our country, but for the world.

"Questions, Mr. Kokk?"

I took the thick folder. "I'll give this material my close attention, Minister. Immediately after I acquire a good bottle of cognac to expedite its study."

The deputy minister smiled as he stood. "The cognac will be delivered to your hotel within the hour."

Dazed but pleased, I stood.

"You'll do this job for us?"

"Depends upon the cognac, Minister."

ELEVEN

AMSTERDAM

Tapping out my little black pipe the next morning, I straightened and slowly climbed the steep marble steps of the van Gogh Museum. Leaving old comrades in The Hague, knowing I might never see any of them again, was wrenching.

Since arriving in Amsterdam and checking into the Conscious Hotel on Museum Square, I'd felt queasy and anxious.

An eerie feeling of being watched and followed haunted me. The wariness couldn't be ignored even though I was in the middle of a big bustling city instead of a canopied jungle in Surinam.

The brilliant morning sunshine, gentle winds and attractive females along the Potterstraat began to cheer me. Frequently pausing to light the pipe, I furtively studied shoppers and traffic.

Yesterday I had been amused at the Deputy Minister's parting remark. "You must treat this assignment as sensitive. So sensitive, I urge you to requisition a firearm from the police in Amsterdam when they brief you."

Today his warning wasn't funny. Taking a breath, I glanced around once again and entered the van Gogh Museum.

"I'm here to meet the museum director," I told the uniformed guard first, then the attractive receptionist.

"My name is Kokk. Jan Kokk." I liked her smile.

"The director is expecting you, Mr. Kokk. Please follow me."

I enjoyed the young lady's lithe movements as I followed her down a hallway to a heavy door where she paused to enter a code.

"Go right in, Mr. Kokk. Director Ruddiker is waiting for you." Either from politeness or security rules she waited to click the door behind me.

I stayed her hand. "Perhaps a drink later? I'll check with you after your director finishes fricasseeing me."

She raised an eyebrow. "Let's hope you pass the tenderness test, Mr. Kokk." With that, she turned on her heel, locking the door behind her.

"Please come in, Mr. Kokk. I'm also a Jan, Doctor Jan Ruddiker, director of the museum." The tall, skeletal graying man extended a flaccid hand, which I took gingerly.

Ruddiker waved me to a chair beside a table already set with tea and biscuits.

"Prefer coffee or tea, Mr. Kokk?"

"Whatever you're having, Director." I sunk into a yielding leather chair.

Ruddiker passed me a cup and saucer. "Please try the *koekjes*," he offered a plate.

"These cookies were baked by the same young lady who is going to summarize van Gogh's last works for you before the two of you depart on your mission."

Unconvinced, I blinked. "Is that really necessary for the investigation of his death, Director?"

Ruddiker removed and polished his glasses before answering. Without spectacles, his bulging eyes reminded me of a goldfish I'd been given as a child.

"There's much to learn about a person's character from his work, Mr. Kokk." He took two cookies.

"Van Gogh's paintings provide valuable insights to his personality, his faults, even likes and dislikes."

I stopped a sneeze. "Excuse me, Director. I understand I am to investigate his death, not his personality."

Ruddiker made a temple of long fingers. "I think you'll find our young lady's observations most useful to your understanding of the painter. Her services will provide you a great advantage in a foreign country. She's an outstanding, talented employee and not only for her baking skills." The director smiled, helping himself to another cookie.

I conceded. "I look forward to her assistance. When do I meet this talented young lady?"

"She's prepared to brief you here tomorrow at one, if that's convenient. I see from the schedule you have morning sessions with the police."

This seemed his signal for me to leave.

Ruddiker sprang up to stand beside the door. "You realize, Mr. Kokk, that your assignment is highly sensitive? There are certain to be people who will vehemently oppose your investigation."

"People in France?"

"Yes. Your findings, when publicized, may be objectionable to our next-door good neighbor. Good bye, Mr. Kokk, and good luck."

At the curb I waved down a taxi and asked the driver to take me to police headquarters. The appointment with a police inspector named van Groot was at ten o'clock. I rechecked my printed schedule marked "CONFIDENTIAL." in red ink.

Inside the sleek, predominately glass structure I followed arrows from the main corridor to a reception desk, my third or fourth of the day.

To myself I grumbled. "I should start counting receptionists. I spend more time with them than anyone in Amsterdam."

"Pardon?" Another female receptionist broke my trance. She blinked eyes so green they must be from contacts.

I admired her pixie short black hair. "Jan Kokk to see Inspector van Groot, if you please."

Another female, this one wearing the uniform of a police cadet, nodded at the receptionist recording my name and time. "This way, Mr. Kokk."

She led me to an elevator, preceded me in and punched the fourth floor button.

"You'll be met at the elevator as you exit." Her accent reminded me of home.

I asked her in Papiamentu. "You from Curacao?"

She smiled brightly. "No, sir. I'm originally from Aruba. You from Curacao?"

As the door closed, I suggested, "Perhaps we can have a coffee when I'm finished upstairs?"

Her only response was another smile as the elevator door closed.

Another cadet, a male this time, met the elevator on the fourth floor and walked me to the appropriate office.

A tall balding man wearing gold crown epaulets stood behind a cluttered desk.

"*Bon dia,* Mr. Kokk. Did I say that correctly in Papamientu? I'm Chief Inspector van Groot. Please have a chair while I ring for coffee. Or would you prefer something stronger at this hour?"

Van Groot's smile exposed shiny gold-rimmed teeth. He winked. "I understand cognac is a favorite?"

I was baffled that he knew that. "Thank you, Inspector. Coffee's fine." His office walls were covered with framed photographs of the Queen reviewing a police parade.

Instead of sitting behind his desk, the inspector took a chair beside mine, regarding me sternly.

Business-like, he began. "I'll be brief, Mr. Kokk. "First, I'm delighted, as is the Chief Commissioner, that you've agreed to take this peculiar assignment."

"Sir, please give the Chief Commissioner my compliments."

"Thank you, Mr. Kokk. I shall.

"Secondly, I must impress you with the confidential nature of this matter. Sending an investigator to a foreign country to inquire about a tragedy that happened years ago could severely impact the good relations developed in that long interim between that country and our own."

Probably I frowned at hearing this again.

"You have reservations, Mr. Kokk?"

"I do, Inspector. If his death was actually the result of suicide--as is commonly presumed--how are the 'good relations' you speak of altered in any way?"

Van Groot ground his molars. "True. If you find our famous Dutchman, of whom we are justly proud, was *murdered*, possibly by a French citizen then that relationship might suffer."

Tempted to pull out my pipe, I resisted. "Sir, that relationship must be very fragile to be damaged by a death occurring 126 years ago."

"True, but our government prefers the matter be handled with due diligence. The French are viable partners in our economic union. We prefer nothing interfere or diminish that."

"Then why bother to investigate van Gogh's death to begin with, Inspector?"

Van Groot clicked his teeth. "Another anniversary of his death is this July. Our government feels it's time that we discover--as discreetly as possible--the facts about our great painter's death.

"That is the assignment which, I'm told, you have accepted?" The inspector's tone was more challenge than question.

I nodded and van Groot silently replenished my coffee.

"Do the French understand and agree to my mission?"

"They do. Were you to ask are they enthusiastic, I'd say not at all. That's why you must proceed with caution."

He turned his attention to a nearby table covered with a large cloth. He stood and removed the cloth.

"Speaking of caution, choose your weapon, Mr. Kokk."

TWELVE

On the table several semiautomatic pistols glistened from recent oiling. "You may need one of these before your mission is over, Mr. Kokk. Which do you prefer?"

I looked them over and selected one. "I like this full-size model," I hefted a pistol.

"The compact models are too small for my hand. I once carried a Glock pistol similar to this one in Surinam."

"Excellent. Would you care to fire a few rounds downstairs in our range? If so, I'll have you escorted there by a constable and ask that you return here later after you're satisfied with the weapon."

Once returned from the firing range, the inspector waved me to the same seat.

He smiled broadly. "Is your pistol satisfactory? I heard that you just tore the bull's eye out of five targets."

I wondered aloud. "How do I sneak it into France?"

Van Groot held out his hand. "We'll pouch it and a box of ammunition to our embassy in Paris. Someone will discreetly deliver them to you at that little hotel in Auvers. I presume that's where you'll stay?"

"Yes sir. I've read the reports, both French and our own. Auvers appears to be the prime--maybe the only important--location. How am I to report progress?"

The inspector's smile faded. "Normally, you won't. The French might intercept any mail, telegram or telephone calls. Simply report to me here once you complete the job. Agreed?"

"What about our embassy in Paris?"

"We prefer you stay away from it as much as possible. Traipsing in and out of that chancery would draw undue attention."

Feeling more secret agent than investigator, I stood to leave.

"Bon chance, Mr. Kokk!"

THIRTEEN

It was a beautiful Amsterdam morning, warm enough to induce locals and tourists to throng the sidewalk cafes, enjoying *koffie* and *appeltaart*. Even the usually dour café waiters in their white shirts, black bow ties and trousers seemed cheery. The sky was a shade of Delft blue almost matching the tableware on my small table.

"Mr. Kokk?"

I looked up from the morning newspaper and blinked. The vision before me epitomized the blonde, blue-eyed young Dutch woman. Although diminutive, her figure was perfect despite the severe business blouse and skirt she chose as camouflage.

I stumbled to rise almost spilling the just-filled coffee. I smiled as never before at this time of day.

"Yes?" I bleated, offering the chair across from mine. "Won't you join me?"

Nodding, she stuck out a gloved hand and gave me a handshake considerably firmer than that of her boss. I knew this vision was my assistant and co-conspirator from the museum. My traveling companion!

She sat down primly, placing her handbag between us in case I leaped. "My name is Susse Thankker, Mr. Kokk. I'm from the van Gogh Museum. Director Ruddiker sent me.

"He spied you sitting here and instructed me to join you. Perhaps I'm intruding? We aren't scheduled to meet until one this afternoon."

"I'm delighted to see you, early or late. You look lovely, much better, I imagine, than any of our famous painter's models."

She laughed, almost relaxing. "I see we have a lot to learn about van Gogh and his models, Mr. Kokk…"

I interrupted. "Jan. Please call me Jan."

She sniffed at the interruption. "His models were not all that attractive, Mr. Kokk." She emphasized the 'mister.'

"Surely we should be friends," I protested. "We must work together--depend upon each other--during a hectic foreign assignment."

I quickly added. "*Closely* together, if we are to be successful."

She tensed. "Since you broached the subject of togetherness, allow me to be plain, Mr. Kokk."

"Jan." I stressed. "Jan."

"I assure you that I will dutifully and *professionally* perform the work required of me."

Her tone was like the icing on a week-old cake, tasty but tough.

I motioned to the leering waiter for more coffee and pastries. "Of course, I look forward to our assignment. Please tell me something about yourself, Susse. Or do you prefer Miss Thankker?"

She wrinkled a petite nose. "You may use either name since I'm your humble working interpreter and assistant."

I leaned forward to better see her remarkable eyes. "I didn't expect such a beautiful colleague. I must send your director a box of Havanas."

She tittered. "He doesn't smoke, sir. You." she straightened in her chair, "must not flatter a poor working Dutch girl."

"Yes," I acknowledged. "I sense an age barrier to overcome."

"Ours will be a working relationship, sir," she reiterated.

We studied each other. Breaking the silence, I offered her a cigarette.

"I don't smoke, Mr. Kokk." She stirred her now tepid coffee.

"Born in Amsterdam?"

She stirred more briskly. "Yes, my family has lived here for years."

"Mother and father?" Absent a wedding ring, I asked anyway. "Husband?"

"Only my parents, Mr. Kokk." Her eyes challenged me to stop asking.

"I'm sure there are many young men--*schats*—-knocking on your door."

"Stop it, Mr. Kokk," she shook her head. "I should question you in the same manner.

"Tell me, does the famous private investigator have a large family awaiting him on lovely Curacao?"

I motioned to the waiter for menus. "Let's first order lunch. I'm starving. You?"

She frowned. "That's a typically selective male response."

I feigned innocence. "Let's declare a truce until afternoon. The fish here is extraordinary. Perhaps a nice dry white wine?"

FOURTEEN

PARIS

Captain Claud Coffier of the Judicial Police, Metropole Division, glared at his glass-fronted door as someone tapped.

"Damn!" he muttered. "It's that Lieutenant Fourange again." For the umpteenth time Coffier vowed he would order the glass replaced by wood. Solid oak, maybe. He wanted a respectable no-nonsense door separating him from the outside. No more constables peeking in as he labored at his mahogany desk.

With a wave, he beckoned the young officer inside.

"Good morning, Captain."

"Good morning," he replied, mind on a work order for the new door. "What exciting news do you bring?"

"Photographs, Captain."

"Of what?"

Hastily Lieutenant Fourange spread several black and whites on his superior's vacant spotless glass-topped desk

"It's him, sir!"

"Who?"

"The man the Dutch are sending to investigate the old suicide of that deranged painter."

Coffier picked up one of the grainy photos and studied it at eye level. "You mean the big fellow? How do you know he's the one?"

Fourange's voice tingled with excitement. "Because these photos were made outside Dutch police headquarters and at the van Gogh Museum on Monday and Tuesday.

"Same man. Both places. He must be the one we are to watch for!"

Coffier chuckled. "Looks like the typical fat tourist to me. Probably touring Amsterdam's sinful delights. Just returned from that famous red-light district. See that smirk on his face?"

Pointing, he chuckled. "Looks satiated, doesn't he?"

Nonplussed, Fourange continued. "Here's another one, sir. Same man at an outdoor café near the van Gogh Museum."

This photo interested the captain. "Who's the good-looker with fatso?"

"No idea as yet. We're checking on her identity, sir. He must be the investigator they wired the Surete about, requesting our assistance."

"Smiling negligence is all they'll get from us. If that's him, that is. Imagine digging up a closed case that old!"

"Sir, I recommend we alert the commissioner and local *maire.*"

"About what?"

"Send them these photos, sir. Tell them this man is coming to snoop into the suicide of that crazy Dutch painter. We should follow his investigation as closely as possible."

"Why?"

With his handkerchief, Fourange dabbed at his forehead. "To avert any false reports, sir. We must be prepared to discredit any finding this foreigner comes up with which is detrimental to French interests."

At the captain's look, he added. "And the Judicial Police, of course."

The captain yawned and waved him out. "Don't rattle the door."

Captain Coffier closed his eyes. The rattle of the glass door was disquieting to his thoughts about the promotion board scheduled to convene next week.

He lit his favorite smoke--a *Gauloise Caporal*--and shrugged. How could a century-old suicide of a demented Dutch painter be of any significance to a promotion board?

"The lieutenant needs a vacation," he said aloud, making a note.

"He's going gah, gah. Delusional."

Coffier smiled. "By the time he returns, I'll have a proper new door."

FIFTEEN

AMSTERDAM

She frowned at her image as she applied mascara and lip gloss in the small hotel mirror. Kokk suggested she move into his hotel "to facilitate our gallery study and departure for Paris."

Sleeping in an unfamiliar hotel bed and hearing unusual noises kept her awake most of the night. Or was it her constant thoughts and worries about Sophie?

Not hearing from her friend since their last telephone call made Susse miserable. Karl's monitoring the home telephones kept Susse from dialing Sophie's private number. The morning newspaper lacked any personal column notices for "Alexis" the *nom de plume* given her by Sophie.

Was Sophie ill or hospitalized? Maybe she was locked in a closet and nightly brutalized by that vicious husband?

"Men!" she spat, smudging the mascara for the second time.

Thoughts shifted to Jan Kokk. Although courteous, something about the oversized investigator, with whom she was supposed to work, disturbed Susse. He coaxed her into moving into his hotel, even on the same floor. Kokk's room was just down the hall from her own.

Adding to her distrust, Kokk delayed accompanying her to the museum to study the selected paintings and hear her carefully prepared discourse on each one. Susse regretted the director had selected her for this assignment with that big, unsettling Caribbean man.

Downstairs, she marched into the dining room where they breakfasted. Would Kokk beg off the museum session again? If so, she would ask Director Ruddiker for relief.

I arose as she came into the dining room and held her chair. "Good morning. I hope you slept well."

"It was a terrible night," she flushed. "I didn't mean that lovely dinner and walk along the canal we had. They were quite relaxing."

I grinned at her look. "That's alright, Susse. I know I'm not the type of escort you normally have in the evenings."

She closed her eyes for a second. "I meant that my sleep was fitful, but not because of our evening together."

She twisted her linen napkin. "I do worry..." She stopped, seeking the right words.

"About?"

"Well, Mr. Kokk..."

"Jan."

"As you prefer. Jan. I'm concerned about my job. If I keep traipsing about Amsterdam with you like a tourist, the director's likely to find someone else to perform my position."

I patted her hand. "I assure you I will prevent your director from firing you. If he did, we'd find you a better job in the Ministry."

She paused, uncertain if he was boasting. "Ministry?"

I patted the hand again. "I thought you knew. We report to the Ministry of Arts and Culture. The Ministry, not the museum, is paying our bills.

"Now," I unfolded the menu. "Let's enjoy a hearty breakfast before we tour the beautiful Keukenhof Gardens."

"Gardens? Oh, no! If I don't get you into the museum today, I'm really in jeopardy."

"I'll explain to the director that I'm new in town. I need to absorb a little of Amsterdam before flying off to a foreign country. Isn't that convincing?"

"You've lived in the Netherlands before. Surely you're no stranger to..."

"The Marechausee training center is outside Utrecht, not here. I never had a chance to see your delightful Amsterdam."

Studying her concerned expression, I suggested "Let's make a pact."

Her concern changed to alarm. "A what?"

"A pact. We tour the Keukenhof Gardens this morning while the flowers are at their best. Then, we spend the whole afternoon in the museum, pleasing you and your director."

That earned her first smile of the morning.

"There is a caveat, however."

I had another proposal for this evening. "Please accompany me to hear the Concertgeboux Orchestra tonight. They're playing excerpts from Beethoven's Fifth and Eighth symphonies."

She rattled the cup and saucer. "I'm surprised that you, a former police man and soldier, care for Beethoven."

Touching her chin, I bragged. "Don't care for surprises? I have others, too."

After the waiters cleared the table she noticed her hand still rested on mine.

"Stunning! Beautiful!" She responded as we returned from touring the famous Keukenhof Gardens.

"Did van Gogh paint lots of flower fields like we just saw?"

"Well," she moistened her lips, "he painted many wheat fields and gardens. Two of them you'll see in the museum. He was very fond of painting flower arrangements, too."

"The real thing's better than a dusty old painting hung on a wall," I suggested. "Right?"

"You're trying to get out of our afternoon at the museum!" She accused, punching my arm. "Just another tricky male!"

"Not at all," I managed. "Since you love art, I knew the gardens would thrill you. I doubt you've ever taken the time to visit those gardens although Amsterdam is your home.

"Am I right?"

Avoiding the question, she directed the cab driver to the van Gogh Museum. "We're not going by the hotel, Jan. We're going directly to the museum. Remember our pact?"

SIXTEEN

Vincent van Gogh

"This way, Jan."

She used my first name. I followed, happy with small victories.

A moment later we stood in the east gallery of the modernistic van Gogh Museum, Susse's workplace.

She pointed to a portrait of an intense, staring, heavily bearded man. The focal point of the painting was his eyes. They seemed to both challenge and follow the viewer.

"This must be Vincent van Gogh. Should I genuflect?"

"Be serious, Jan."

"Remind me again why we're here."

Lips set tightly, she stepped in front of the painting. "I want to familiarize you with the work of the man whose death we go to investigate. There's much to learn about this unusual individual from his masterpieces.

"I intend to prepare you for your work by repeating what many art critics think his paintings reveal."

"Were his hair and beard really red or is that artistic license?"

"Really red. He painted lots of self-portraits like this one during his lifetime. I've heard there are at least thirty-five self-portraits, depicting him in different moods, clothing and, of course, varying ages.

"This one was done in September 1889. The next May he moved to Auvers-sur-Oise where he painted until his death in July of that year."

"Why did he paint himself so often?"

"Probably to experiment with the different light patterns and brush strokes. Often he was the most available, certainly the cheapest, model."

Frowning, I began. "To me, he looks both desperate and angry. Certainly not a happy man."

Susse pointed to a bench in the middle of the room. "Let's sit for a moment. I'm sure you know he suffered from bouts of deep depression throughout his life. He was institutionalized--as they now call it--many times.

"Have you read much about him, Jan?"

"Not guilty, Professor."

"Well, he left an asylum at St. Remy, went to Paris for a time, then moved to Auvers. In Auvers he could be under the care of a local doctor named Gachet. Vincent was not only Gachet's patient. They became friends and spent much time together, usually in the doctor's home. Eventually their friendship seemed to change for some reason."

Pensive, I wanted to hear again why I was there. "How does what you just told me have any bearing on a factual investigation?"

She brushed a lock of blonde hair aside. "Although he was a troubled man, he actively sought help to restore normalcy. Just like yours and mine, his life was often difficult and unpleasant. He tried to deal with his malady rather admirably I'd say."

She stood, beckoning me further down the hall. "I apologize, Mr. Kokk. I was unable to arrange the pieces I've selected to discuss with you in their proper order. We must skip around the museum a bit."

She called me 'Mister,' again. Did I irritate?

"This next piece," she stepped ahead of me down another corridor, "is very significant."

Halting in front of a much smaller painting, she pointed. "This painting, called 'Two Lovers,' is just a fragment of his larger work. I prefer this little one because it epitomizes his loneliness and desire for female companionship. I think he desperately envied the couple you see in this painting."

Two Lovers

I studied this painting. Clinging tightly to each other I saw the backsides of an elderly couple trudging down a small path away from me.

"Except for the bright colors, it could be you and I going to the Concertgeboux tonight," I kidded.

She pursed her lips. "Can't you feel the painter's terrible loneliness and desire for companionship from this work?"

"Didn't he have many lady friends? I thought all artists had plenty of female admirers."

"Not van Gogh," she exhaled. "He pursued love many times without success. An early example was a tragic affair he had in London."

"He lived in London?"

"Several times. While living in South London, he fell in love with the redheaded daughter of his landlady. After months of adoring her from a distance, he worked up the courage to tell her of his feelings. The daughter, Eugenie, flatly rejected him.

"Unknown to van Gogh, Eugenie had become engaged to another man who also lodged there before Vincent. That failed attempt to offer himself to Eugenie left a lasting and humiliating mark from which van Gogh never recovered."

She studied me. "Tell me, Jan. How do you suppose *you* would have reacted?"

I touched her free hand. "I'd be very persistent, yet patient. Just like now." I kissed her palm.

Blushing, Susse jerked her hand away, using it to turn another page in the notebook.

She took a deep breath. "You never answered my question, Jan."

"What question?"

"Remember? I asked you about your family in Curacao. Is it a large one?"

"Like your painter here," I gestured at his rendition of the two elderly lovers, "I'm alone.

"Failure doesn't deter me. I'm still searching for the right lady."

Quickly turning away, she strode to another painting. "This is a famous painting of some of the houses in Auvers. First, I should show you Auvers-sur-Oise on the map."

She sat on another bench, unfolding a road map of Paris and vicinity. "Here's where we're going," she pointed. "Auvers is just a small country village less than 20 miles northwest of Paris.

"See it?"

Nodding, I looked from the map to the new painting. "Looks like a quiet, thatch-roofed, peaceful place. There's that orange color again," I pointed. "One of his favorites?"

"You're right, although he'd probably call it ochre. See anything else?"

I looked again. "You want me to say something about that lonely figure, looks like male, walking alone between those houses."

"That's perceptive, Jan," she effused. "This speaks again of van Gogh's loneliness, doesn't it?

"Does Auvers look like a quaint, placid little village?"

"Yes, Professor," I teased. "I look forward to visiting it with you."

"Would you say it appears to be a place to go for healing rather than harm?"

I regarded her playfully. "You're multi-talented, lady, a beauty and a psychologist, too!"

She snapped shut the notebook. "Don't humor me, Mr. Kokk. Perhaps it's time we leave if you're still intent on hearing Beethoven this evening."

Houses in Auvers

SEVENTEEN

"ALEXIS: MY NEW JOB REQUIRES I GO TO FRANCE.
MEET ME TOMORROW AT OUR USUAL PLACE/TIME. I
MUST SEE YOU."

Susse reread the advertisement she'd just rewritten for the third
time. Not hearing from Sophie, *she* was initiating the advertisement in
the personal section of the morning paper.

"I must see her before I leave," Susse repeated to herself. "I need to
know she's all right or I can't leave Amsterdam."

Susse needed physical assurance to renew her feelings toward Sophie.
A tinge of guilt nagged. Should she tell Sophie about the strange man
she must accompany to France?

"I'm not sure I should mention Jan," she confessed aloud.

She finished brushing hair and applying makeup before meeting
Kokk in the hotel bar. On the way downstairs she'd mail the
advertisement to the newspaper, hoping—-no, praying--that Sophie
would see it and comply.

"I must see her!" She said it again as she stepped out of the elevator,
asking the desk clerk to mail the letter to the newspaper.

Outside, I held an umbrella for Susse as we entered a taxi bound for
the concert hall. Despite the rain—-first sprinkling, then soaking--the
streets were full of vehicles and people hurrying home. The concert hall's
street, *Museumplein*, was even worse.

Susse seemed preoccupied so I sat quietly during our cab ride to the
famous old concert hall. From a distance it looked like an elaborately
decorated birthday cake.

Mounting concerns absorbed Susse's thoughts

Will my advertisement reach the newspaper in time for the morning edition? Will Sophie see my ad? Can she meet me at the oyster restaurant or must I return to the hotel further depressed and lonely?

The concert hall's entrance and main floor were very crowded. I guided her upstairs to our seats in the front balcony. "The acoustics are much better up here," I claimed.

We sat, facing a gigantic pipe organ looming over the concert orchestra. Although the instrument was silent, its immensity was hypnotic.

Once the music began, the trance lifted and Susse's thoughts returned to Sophie.

If I don't hear from Sophie should I refuse to go to France with Kokk? Could a claim of sudden illness excuse me from the trip? Would I lose my new job if I fail to accompany him?

She hardly seemed to hear the music. I nudged her at intermission and she jumped at my touch.

"Let's go to the mezzanine for champagne," I suggested. "Shall we?"

The chilled *brut* seemed to ease her anxieties for a moment. She responded easily to my question about the performance.

"Splendid. Remarkable, I thought." She turned the question. "What about you, Jan?"

With gestures about the contrasting movements and the *allegro con brio,* I tried to interest her. The champagne seemed to enliven her more than my antics. When we started to our seats upstairs, her funk returned.

Do I really want to accompany this strange man to tiny Auvers for an open-ended stay? Can I withstand his persistence and obvious interest? How long?

As the performance ended we drank more champagne. My excuse was we should allow the crush of music lovers to diminish before we left. We clinked glasses until the champagne bottle was empty.

"I'm surprised you're an avid classical music fan, Jan. That seems unusual for a private investigator."

I joked. "They even play Beethoven in the zoo to calm the animals at night. In Surinam classical music was all we could receive over the local station. I learned to love it."

In the taxi back seat Susse politely evaded my encircling arm. Me, the gallery, her explanation of the paintings and the crowded concert sapped her energy. As expected she claimed exhaustion once we walked into the hotel.

She cut short my invitation for a nightcap in the hotel bar. "Until tomorrow, Jan. Thank you for another marvelous evening."

Minutes later I occupied a barstool by myself. "Alone," I complained, "just like that famous Dutch painter."

EIGHTEEN

I fumbled with my pipe, puzzled why Susse was so quiet at breakfast. She seemed in a world of her own, incessantly toying with the classified pages of the morning *Telegraaff.*

"Something wrong with your eggs and sausage?" Usually her appetite was as keen as mine.

"No, no. Everything's fine." The words failed to hide her obvious distress. She dabbed at her eyes with a napkin.

All the way to the museum she remained quiet, staring at the wrinkled newspaper she clutched. At the museum I opened the taxi door and offered her my hand.

Then I saw the man staring at us on the sidewalk near our taxi.

Suddenly I hissed "Cover your face!" as she stood beside me at the open door of the cab.

The stranger aimed a camera at us. "Hide your face!" I repeated.

Shocked, Susse stared at me, still facing the man.

I grabbed and kissed her, shielding her face with my shoulder.

Angrily, she slapped me hard. The man with the camera scurried to the opposite corner and was briskly walking away. Hopefully he would be disappointed with the fuzzy, blurred photograph he'd just made of us.

I hustled Susse through the museum entrance. "I'll explain inside."

"You brute!" She hit me with a fist. "What makes you think you could get away with that?"

I guided her toward the vacant staff lounge. "Let's have a coffee while I explain."

Enraged, she hit me again as I tried to seat her in the lounge.

"Another male animal!" She screeched, "I expected more from you, Mr. Kokk!"

Balancing two filled cups from the coffee urn, I sat down opposite her. "Calm down and listen to me, Susse. That wasn't what you thought.

"A man aimed his camera at us as we got out of the taxi. My instinct says he's somehow involved in our investigation. That's why he wanted our photo."

"You wouldn't hide your face as I asked. I had to shield you somehow."

Grinning, I boasted, "I succeeded!"

The explanation seemed shallow, even to me. I sipped the hot coffee. "I apologize for startling you."

She stared at me for minutes, which seemed much longer.

"You enjoyed it," she accused. "Didn't you?"

"I intend to protect you, Susse, whether you like it or not."

She huffed. "I didn't see any danger. That man was probably just a tourist photographing the famous van Gogh Museum."

I blew on my hot coffee. "Then why did he bugger away, almost running?"

She shrugged, unconvinced. "You're very adept at avoiding answering simple questions, like about your mysterious family."

My cup slipped, spilling coffee. "I told you I have no family."

Her eyes still blazed. "Did you enjoy abusing me?"

With a napkin I wiped up the spill. "Immensely. The next time the kiss will be no surprise and much longer."

She opened her notebook and bent over a page. "There won't be a next time, Mr. Kokk. I remind you, we are professionals conducting an important official investigation."

She shrugged. "Speaking of that, we need to get started. We've only tomorrow to finish and be on our way to Auvers."

She stared at me again. "That is, if I choose to go with you after that arrogant macho display."

Coming around the corner, Ruddiker, the museum director, spotted us. "All going well?"

"Fine, Mr. Ruddiker," I replied before Susse could. "My fondest expectations are being exceeded."

Village Street in Auvers

Walking down a familiar corridor, Susse stopped before another painting. "This one's entitled 'Village Street in Auvers.' It again depicts the peaceful French village where van Gogh chose to live and work."

"And recuperate?"

"Exactly, Mr. Kokk. He chose Auvers not just for the atmosphere but to be under the care of a local physician, Dr. Gachet, whom I mentioned before. Remember?"

I nodded. "Still, I see little nexus between the painter's geographical preference and our investigation of his death.

"Do you think we can finish my tutorials by tomorrow evening?" I wondered.

"Probably." She overlooked the sarcasm. "Only if you act maturely."

She referred to her notes. "Let's examine this painting. It depicts a quiet cluster of country cottages. Auvers then had a population of perhaps 2,000 souls, mostly farmers and trades people. Today the village boasts of some 7,000 inhabitants. Lots of them are involved in the tourism industry sparked by van Gogh.

"Tell me what you notice in this painting."

"That's easy," I yawned. "He likes that orange--or as you prefer--ochre color. Is there a reason the trees and the clouds are misshapen? The street is deserted. Looks very lonely: there's that word again."

"Exactly." She raised her arms in victory. "That's how his clouded mind envisioned the skeletal trees and odd clouds. He's alone, so he paints the narrow, vacant little street to reflect his feeling."

She stepped across the corridor to another painting. "Here Vincent was not alone. He was with another person--a woman--and must have enjoyed being with her."

"Who's she?"

"She is Marguerite Gachet, daughter of the physician treating Vincent's melancholy. She's playing the piano in the Gachet home. I can imagine that the music, her dress--even her scent--enthralled the painter. Can't you?"

"Yes, Professor," I concurred. "It seems like a happy scene. When was it painted?"

"Excellent question, Jan." She reverted to my given name. "It was painted in June, the month before his death.

"She was also the subject of another of his works. It was of Marguerite standing in the Gachet garden wearing a sun hat and filmy dress. It was also painted in June."

"Was she more than his favorite subject?"

Susse lifted eyebrows in response. "I think you begin to see the value of my so-called 'tutorials.' This happy scene reveals something of the painter, doesn't it?"

I admired Susse's persistence. "If I agree, may we go to lunch?"

She checked her wristwatch. "Only if you like oysters."

Marguerite Gachet at the Piano

NINETEEN

Her euphoria vanished as we entered the distant restaurant she selected. *De Oesterbar* was crowded with seafood lovers, most of them gulping raw oysters and clams at the large brass serving bar.

The size of the menu equaled that of the crowd surrounding the bar. I watched her look around the entire room.

"One of your favorite places for lunch?"

Instead of studying the menu, Susse surveyed the customers, looking for someone.

Her expression tensed. "No, I can't afford to come here often but it serves a great variety of seafood. I hope you approve of oysters?"

"Being from the Caribbean, I love seafood."

We sat at a small table and settled on a dry white wine. After sampling it, she ordered a Dover sole. I chose a croquette of shrimp.

"Please excuse me," I stood. "I must make one of those sooner-the-better telephone calls."

She tapped her cell phone. "Use mine. Unless, of course, you're scheduling a midnight rendezvous with a young--or older--woman.

"Go ahead," she urged. "I'd be amused rather than jealous."

Surprised at her last word, I blinked. "It's to the police. I want to report that man taking our photo outside the museum."

"You're serious?"

"Yes, dear lady. I am."

"My phone won't do?"

I leaned forward to pat her hand. "Your phone may be monitored by the same people who hired the cameraman. I'll be back before lunch arrives."

In minutes I returned after relating the incident and my suspicions to Inspector van Groot. He said he appreciated my report. His tone said otherwise.

"Was it one of your men, Inspector?" I asked. Knowing several police inspectors back home, I didn't expect an answer.

His reply was gruff. "If I find out anything, I'll let you know."

I wandered back through the crowd to the table just as our food arrived. "Smells and looks wonderful."

"What did the police say?"

"Noncommittal."

"Could the police be shadowing you, Jan Kokk?"

There was now a long line of customers waiting for tables. She eyed the line carefully.

"Looking for a boyfriend?" I chided, trying to match her rendezvous question.

She ignored me, concentrating on the sole.

A new thought made her look up. "Did you really call the police? Or was that a ruse to make me believe your story about the man with the camera?"

"Honest." I speared a shrimp.

Several times I turned to look out the back window as our taxi returned us to the museum.

After my second or third look, she spoke. "Really, Jan. You are spooking me.

"Tell me the truth. Are we in some kind of danger because of you or because of our assignment?"

Proposing another pact, I countered. "I'll answer *you* if you tell *me* what's been bothering you since breakfast."

She shook her head. "Maybe another time. If and when I feel I can trust you. Really trust you."

"That may be too late for both of us, innocent, engaging Susse."

TWENTY

That afternoon we continued trolling the corridors of the museum, stopping when she pointed out a painting and opened her notebook.

"That looks like a French bordello."

She giggled. "Hotel, Jan. It's a hotel. That's the *Auberge Ravoux* where we're staying in Auvers. We have reservations there in the very place van Gogh lived and died. Exciting?

"He explored the whole countryside around Auvers, happily painting everything which caught his eye."

"You're saying he was a happy lodger at that unimpressive establishment? Does it have running water and electricity?

Ravoux Inn

Pointing at the painting, I said "I bet the Ministry booked us into that hovel."

Giggle gone, she frowned. "No, Jan. I did. Maybe it lacks cable TV and Starbucks but it's a clean, comfortable place to stay. I thought you'd prefer it to the modern plastic Holiday Inn several miles away."

She pressed her advantage. "This is where van Gogh lived during his months in Auvers. You may even get the room in which he died, where he uttered his last words. This little inn may abound in clues, Jan!"

I wanted to ask 'Even after more than a hundred years?' but thought better of it. Her determined chin reminded me of a bill collector.

"Okay," I caved. "It will be fine. Are our rooms adjoining?"

"Definitely not, but close enough for professional communication."

I remembered the question I should have asked earlier. "What about typing and dictation? I'll have to prepare a final report for the Ministry. My longhand is atrocious."

"I got high passes in school. You haven't even asked about my French."

I tried to look apologetic. "Fluent?"

"Yes, Mr. Kokk, fluent. I'm very well qualified to be your associate."

Every time she called me 'Mister,' her irritation buzzed like a mosquito. To divert her ire, I asked, "What's next?"

Adeline Ravoux

Susse pointed to a small frame opposite the painting of the spartan-looking *Auberge Ravoux* where we would stay.

"Here is van Gogh's rendition of another female. This young girl is Adeline Ravoux, daughter of the owner of van Gogh's inn. Her many statements about his death are in all those police reports you carry in that big leather valise with the cognac."

Surprised, I asked, "You read them all?"

"Of course. The police thought I should if I am to assist the mighty investigator. If you overlook a detail in the old reports," she smiled, "I'll remind you."

I stared at the small, unfinished portrait of a young girl posed in an old-fashioned parlor chair. "She looks both virginal and unhappy.

"Did she and Vincent have a 'relationship'? Did she turn him down as did that redhead daughter of his London landlady?"

She sighed. "I don't know. You're getting ahead of yourself. We haven't even finished in this hallway, this museum," she stamped her foot, "here in Amsterdam."

I took a last look at the small portrait of Adeline Ravoux. Had the father asked van Gogh to paint his young daughter? Maybe the painting was in lieu of Vincent's delinquent rent.

"Next?" I prompted.

She already stood before a larger painting, gesturing.

"You may think this one redundant. It's another Auvers scene, this one is titled 'Village Street and Steps.'

"It evokes feelings of peace and serenity, doesn't it?"

I agreed. "Yes, Professor. You've convinced me that Auvers is a magical place, a French version of a kinder, gentler Camelot. This scene looks busy. Plenty of people available to combat our painter's loneliness, right?"

Exasperated, she turned sharply and marched toward the entrance. "We might as well stop for the day. Apparently you find my comments either boring or humorous. Shall we go?"

Village Street and Steps in Auvers

61

I apologize once we were back at the hotel. "Let's have a drink in the bar while I attempt to make amends."

She nodded emphatically. "Yes, we need a serious conversation. I'm not sure I should accompany you to France because of personal issues."

"If I caused them," I felt for my pipe, "I again apologize. I definitely need your help to complete this investigation."

I felt--hopefully looked--contrite. "I can't do it without you, Susse."

She closed her eyes momentarily. "Can I trust you, Jan Kokk? I mean, implicitly trust you?"

"Yes!"

She pulled a tissue from her purse. "I'll first need a double something."

Going to the counter, I asked the bartender for appropriate drinks. After a double or two, I become a wonderful, thoughtful, considerate counselor.

An hour later the mood was amiable. Susse seemed to regard the world--with the help of double gins--as her special oyster. "Funny, neither of us opted for oysters at that restaurant.

"I need to return there tomorrow by 2:00 in hopes of meeting my friend."

"He must be a special friend."

"Yes, Jan, a special friend named Sophie."

I blinked at the gender message. "How do you know she'll be there? It was Sophie you were looking for today?"

"Yes, Mr. Sleuth. She didn't show. I ran another advertisement, asking her to meet me at the oyster bar in tomorrow morning's paper."

I caught the bartender's eye and gestured for another round. "May I accompany you tomorrow? I'll keep my distance if and when your 'special friend' appears."

"I hope to God she does!" Susse effused. "I don't want to leave Amsterdam without seeing her...without knowing."

I couldn't resist. "Knowing what?"

"You're a master interrogator, Jan Kokk. Soon you'll know all my little secrets. Do you despise me?"

I sipped the new drink. "Just trying to be helpful. I'm at least a discrete interrogator. As they say in those American detective stories, 'Mums the Word.'"

She blinked at her empty glass. "I should not be drinking doubles with my...my boss."

"We're a team, together investigating an intriguing historical death."

"What's the phrase you just used?" Her question came out slightly slurred.

"It means your secrets are my secrets. Maybe you should tell me the whole story about Sophie."

Nodding, she sipped her gin. "You already think less of your associate, don't you?"

"Not so. I want you on that Paris airplane with me tomorrow. I don't want you to back out because of this problem. Tell me about it. I'll help."

She took another sip, watching me warily. "We're lovers, Sophie and I. Her husband is the classic male abuser. He recently discovered us together in their home. Now he hates me and takes his anger out on her."

'Recently' sounded like 'resinnly.' "He abuses her and keeps you apart?"

She grabbed my hand. "Exactly, Jan. I can't go to France with you unless I know she's all right."

"That's why you advertised about meeting her at 2:00 at *De Oesterbar?*"

"Exactly."

The last word came out 'zackly.' "Here's what we do," I warmed to my counselor role.

"We go to the museum in the morning and you finish telling me about the remaining paintings you selected.

"Then we lunch at the oyster bar, waiting for her to show. If she doesn't appear..."

I hesitated because Susse began sobbing.

"If she doesn't come, we drive to her home, I knock on the door and ask for her."

Alarmed, Susse looked up. "Her husband would kill you!"

"He's probably at work, right? If she's there, you'll see her and have a tete-a-tete while I sit in the taxi."

TWENTY ONE

At breakfast the next morning, Susse grabbed a newspaper and happily found her second advertisement. She was breathless all the way to the museum.

Standing in another corridor with her open notebook, she became brisk and professional. "I want you to study this painting of the church at Auvers. He painted this masterpiece just a month before his death.

"What do you think of van Gogh's church? What's the message here?"

Church in Auvers

I stepped closer to the canvas. It looked like an ancient church stretching toward the heavens as if pleading for rescue.

"I see what's probably an old decaying church. Through the eyes of a demented painter it must have looked angry. The foreboding clouds obscure the sky. There's more of that ochre paint.

"I take it Vincent was a religious person?"

"Very perceptive, Jan." She patted me. "Yes, I think he was religious."

I probed. "So much so that suicide would be a mortal sin and out of question?"

"You're getting ahead of yourself again."

She stepped into a new corridor and beckoned me to follow. Arms akimbo, she watched me approach then checked her watch. She was anxious to leave for her hoped rendezvous at *De Oesterbar*.

Daubigny's Garden

"Here's another painting which almost cries aloud. Serenity! This one is entitled 'Daubigny's Garden.' Van Gogh admired the work of fellow-painter Charles-Francois Daubigny, who lived in Auvers twenty years before van Gogh moved there. Daubigny died in the 1870s.

"Comment?"

I shrugged. "It's a pleasant view of a garden in bloom. Painted when?"

"In July 1890. This may have been van Gogh's last painting. Experts aren't in agreement about that. Van Gogh regarded gardens, flowers--especially sunflowers--trees and the sun as expressions of the vitality of life."

She touched me again. "Could he have absorbed some of this garden's vitality as he painted it?"

I didn't answer her as she quickly moved to another painting.

"This one's called 'Wheat Field with Crows.' Do you like it? What do you see there?"

"A field of grain ready for harvest."

"What else?"

"Although ripe for harvest, those black clouds…. Are those rain storms in the midst of the menacing clouds? The threatening clouds prevent the threshing of the wheat."

"I think you're right about the two rain storms. Wouldn't the rain and clouds ruin the crop of wheat? Will the grains be ripped off the stalks and be blown away with those menacing crows?"

We stepped back and looked at the painting from a distance.

Finally, I prompted. "Don't tell me this was the work of a happy, well-adjusted person, I see danger and malice in this canvas."

"I agree. This one almost makes me shiver. In the past some experts believed this was Vincent's last work. Early biographers imagined this was the wheat field where van Gogh was shot. That made them think this was his last painting. But it wasn't."

Wheat Field with Crows

She bent over to straighten her hose before looking up at me.

"Poor Jan! Are you absorbing all this? Be strong! We've only one more painting to talk about and this one's it."

She pointed her notebook to a large painting further down the hall. "This is a charming domestic scene called 'Thatched Sandstone Cottages in Chaponval.' Chaponval is a neighboring hamlet west of Auvers.

"On the ladder a man replaces the damaged thatch of his cottage. On the street below, two young people are talking.

Thatched Sandstone Cottages in Chaponval

"As I mentioned, experts on the painter and his works disagree. This painting was also done in July, the month van Gogh was mortally wounded by that pistol shot.

"Do you remember the other painting reputed to be his last?"

"You said it was the one done in the garden of the painter whom Vincent admired. His name escapes me."

"Daubigny."

"Thank you."

"Very good, Jan," she almost purred. "You *have* been paying attention to your 'Professor,' as you labeled and libeled me.

"As promised, this concludes my selection of a few of Vincent's last paintings to show you. I hope they give you a glimmer of the complicated man whose death we go to Auvers to research."

I bowed slightly. "Thank you for your efforts to educate this poor investigator from the far Caribbean. Shall we head for that oyster bar to see if your friend shows up?"

We left the museum and hailed a taxi.

TWENTY TWO

It was almost three in the afternoon. Sophie should have been there by two. Again near tears Susse stared at the restaurant entrance, holding her breath each time the doors opened.

"How about more wine?" I offered.

Imploring, she grabbed my hand. "Do you think she's coming? Maybe she's simply late?"

Her grip was firm and pleasant so I left my hand there. "Let's wait until four then drive by her place."

At four I checked my gold pocket watch and passed her my handkerchief since she was out of tissue.

"I think it's time we go check her home."

Submissive, Susse followed me outside to the taxi stand. She gave the driver an address in an upscale neighborhood where we halted in front of an elegant, two story house minutes later.

I got out, stepping up to a heavy oaken door and pulled the chain.

I waited several moments, then rang again. Looking over my shoulder I checked Susse. She was supposed to be slumped in the taxi, not visible in case Sophie's husband answered the door.

I rang again. This time the door opened slowly revealing an elderly maid dressed primly in gray and white.

She stared at me through the partially open door.

"Not buying," she announced, starting to close the door.

"I'm looking for Mrs. Gogen." I pushed on the closing door. "Is she in?"

"Who are you?"

"I'm her cousin from Utrecht," I lied. "Is she at home?"

The maid was more suspicious than ever. "The mistress never mentioned relatives in Utrecht," she tried again to slam the door.

"I think Cousin Sophie would be very angry if you turned me away."

The name seemed to reassure her. "Well, she's not at home, sir."

"Then tell me when she'll return so I may come again to see her."

"She and her husband left Monday for Majorca. Be gone two weeks."

I thanked the woman and got back in the taxi.

"You can sit up now," I told Susse. "Sophie's not here. The maid says she and that husband have gone to Majorca for two weeks."

"Oh no!" Clenching her fists, she beat on my chest. "That's terrible! What can I do?"

"Let's concentrate on our job. If we work hard, we can be back before she returns."

Head in her hands, she sobbed. "I can't afford to lose this new job. Looks like I must go with you."

I hugged her like the proverbial Dutch uncle and patted her tousled blonde head. "You'll be fine. We'll be back before you know it."

The KLM flight to Paris was typically Dutch: pleasant, efficient and uneventful. Once through customs, Susse's outlook improved. She began complaining about the price of our roundtrip airfares.

"Air France would have been cheaper but the Ministry insisted on KLM." She wrinkled her nose like a housewife selecting fresh fruit.

Soon we were on the A13 highway, out of the Charles De Gaul Airport and heading to the northwest in our just-rented car. The morning sun shone brightly. Susse seemed to relax at the sight of farmland and meadows as we put Paris behind us.

Removing the map from the pocket of our rental Renault, she became the navigator.

"Stay on the A13, toward Val d'Oise," she directed. "In ten miles or so, we should hit A115 toward Pontoise. By the way, that's the nearest police station to Auvers."

"I know." Driving a powerful sedan through the French countryside seemed curative. "Inspector van Groot told me. He also warned that we might be followed from the airport."

I checked the rearview mirror again. "He was right."

"About what?"

"We're being followed. No, don't look around. What's the harm? They know where we're going."

"Who's they? The police?"

Nodding, I pointed at a sign advertising a restaurant a few miles farther. The flight from Amsterdam had been too short for meal service. I was ravenous.

"Hungry? Shall we stop for *dejeuner?*"

She laughed for the first time in several days. "Better leave the French to me, Jan. Your accent is so bad the waiter would charge us double."

Inside, the restaurant looked like an advertisement from *Country Living*. Heavy wooden rafter beams, darkened with age and a fireplace capable of roasting a cow dominated the room. Tables and chairs looked hand hewn, scrubbed shiny. White starched tablecloths and napkins festooned the small tables in the dining area.

After studying the chalkboard menu Susse suggested the daily special, fortified by a house wine and cheese. She demonstrated her fluency not only by ordering our lunch but chatting with the gray-haired waiter about (I presumed) the weather.

"Your accent is as fabulous as that extraordinary chicken," I commended her after sopping the remaining gravy with a hunk of bread. "What is it by the way?"

"*Coq au vin,*" she said. "A required phrase for your first French lesson.

"Repeat after me. *Coq au vin.*"

Fifteen minutes later we crossed the Oise River and turned west. She was still giggling at my attempts to replicate her "*coq au vin.*"

"There, Jan, there," she pointed. "That's the famous *Auberge Ravoux* where we're staying. Parking is in the rear."

Her knowledge of the several interchanges, routes, the hotel and now the parking lot intrigued me. She's been here before? I wondered.

Our smiling host, Maurice Deign, nodded as he looked in his reservations folio. He was a short, balding man with a fringe of reddish hair reminiscent of van Gogh's fiery beard.

"Ah, yes." He acknowledged with a shake of his head, then asked that we sign the old-fashioned register.

Reversing the register on the counter he adjusted his glasses, peering at our signatures. Then, with another shake of his head, "I need your passports, please."

In unison we asked "Why? We're all European Union."

He shrugged. "For the *Commissariate.*"

Ignoring our surprise, he announced our rooms were numbers 8 and 9. Upstairs, he gestured, as he took charge of our passports.

"I wonder if he's somehow related to the Ravoux family who owned this place at the time of van Gogh's death?"

I paused on the stairs with her heavy suitcase. "Perhaps. Did you notice that red hair?"

She sniffed at my remark. "What a suggestion, Jan. You think he and Vincent may be related?"

At the head of the stairs, she realized our rooms were side by side. Her anger was evident.

"I'm going downstairs to demand a room *not* next to yours." She turned to go as I held her back.

"Ours are the last two vacant rooms in this place. Maurice, our host, told me while you were looking at the dining room.

"Side-by-side rooms will make report writing and transcription much more convenient," I wheedled.

She glowered. "Convenience is not part of our contract, Mr. Kokk. There better be a thick locked door between us."

TWENTY THREE

After unpacking, I suggested we prepare a work place in my room near our common door, which indeed proved stout and lockable.

Susse watched as I moved a dressing table, the only item in my spartan little room except a bed and chair, toward our dividing door.

"I wonder," I began, "if this could be the tiny room where our painter lived? If so, I can understand his jaundiced view of life."

She brushed aside the sarcasm in favor of a question. "Do you understand clearly, Mr. Kokk?"

I stopped maneuvering the dressing table and arranging two chairs beside it.

"Does Mr. Kokk understand what?" I chided her for calling me 'Mister.'

"You are not to enter my room at anytime for any reason whatsoever."

"Of course," I answered. "Unless I'm invited."

"That's fantasy, *not* reality. I'm serious, Jan."

I paraphrased her usual pronouncement. "Ours is a professional relationship. We're here together to solve an old mystery with far-reaching consequences for both history and art.

"Does that about summarize it?"

Encouraged by her nod, I continued. "Then bring your pencils, pads and what-not in here ready for use. I don't intend that this hundred-year-old mystery requires more than a few days working in this elegant five-star hotel you selected.

"Then we'll be back in Amsterdam," I smiled. "You can joke with Sophie about the terrors of being alone with a Caribbean man."

Susse crossed her arms. "You can be very cryptic, Jan Kokk."

"I just wanted to emphasize our pact."

Seated at the desk, I looked up. "I don't recall. Did the pact prohibit our enjoying our work?"

Placing the almost-full bottle of cognac on the table, I motioned. "Please bring your bathroom glass here and let's have a small toast to success before we descend to supper and meet the cast of our mystery theatre."

The hotel's evening meal was served family-style at a large oval table. We sat in the dining room adjoining the vestibule where we'd surrendered our passports.

Maurice Deign, now dressed in white shirt and black trousers, greeted us and began introducing the other diners staring at us from around the table.

They seemed to view Susse and I as interlopers, here for no possible legitimate purpose in this cozy village they discovered first.

Absently, I offered our names.

"This is my wife, Tania, and," he extended his arm to another female "our daughter Mara."

Tania, his elderly wife, looked apprehensive but doffed her head in greeting. She wore a too-small flowery floor-length housecoat. Half-smiling, Tania's teeth clattered.

"Our daughter Mara," she repeated, gesturing. Mara Deign was a slightly stout, over-fifty female with short auburn-hair and penetrating hazel eyes. Seeming to calculate our weight or worth, the unsmiling daughter stared at us before retreating into the kitchen.

Moving down the table, Maurice indicated a solemn looking older couple, both dressed in depressing black. "This is Mr. and Mrs. Schenk from Alsace-Lorraine, visiting here."

Deign added, "We have many visitors interested in the many famous painters who lived and worked in Auvers."

"Are you tourists like the rest of us?"

The question came from a well-dressed young man sitting at the far end of the table. He adjusted round glasses to examine us more clearly. Dark-haired, he fingered his thin gray stubble. Obviously pleased with Susse, he arose and bowed.

"I am Louis Monoud. I'm here finishing my dissertation about the famous Auvers church."

Raising bushy eyebrows, he lectured. "The church was immortalized, you know, by Vincent van Gogh who once lived in this very establishment."

Both Susse and I nodded, replying almost in unison: "Yes, we've heard of the famous painter."

Monoud smiled. "You're Dutch?"

"Yes," I answered first. "And you?"

After an exaggerated smile, "I am French of course."

TWENTY FOUR

After a simple dinner of fish and creamed vegetables, Susse and I excused our selves and took a stroll about the village. Our hotel seemed centrally located on Place de la Maire so we started off down the main street to the west.

"What did you think of those characters back there?"

She hissed. "That young Frenchman on the end is frightening. Did you see him leer at me as we left?"

"He finds you very attractive. Surely you've encountered that many times. I totally agree with him."

She stopped short. "Agree with what? That you find him sinister?"

"That I find you most attractive." We reached a cross street marked Vue Carnet. "Shall we sit for a moment?" I pointed to a painted wooden bench on the corner.

She sat, reproaching me. "Yes, I've been told that a few times, Mr. Kokk. I'm unimpressed and prefer you not repeat it. As you know, I have a dear, close friend in Amsterdam named Sophie."

"I'll remember," I cajoled. "Back to business. I think our conversations about our work should be limited to the outdoors, like this."

She chuckled. "Next you'll tell me that Tania Deign is a paid agent of the Surete here to spy on us."

"I'd wager someone at the inn has been recruited to report our activities. You and I must share everything. With the others, we should be close-mouthed about this case and what we're doing."

"I know that, Jan. The Ministry made that very clear. How do we safeguard drafts of the report?"

Having no ready solution, I sighed. "Don't know. We can't trust our papers to the hotel safe if there is one. What do you think?"

Beaming, she flipped open her notebook. "I think my unusual shorthand is unreadable to anyone but myself. I'll keep this steno pad with me at all times, under my pillow at night."

"Fine, let's try that," I agreed, wondering if I'd ever share that pillow. Her sharp question routed my thought. "Where do we begin?"

"It might be useful for us separately to speak to Maurice and Tania this evening. I'll ask him where are the best fishing places on the river and where to buy fishing gear. I presume we'll need fishing licenses as well."

"We're posing as fisher folk?"

I shrugged. "We'll cause less attention if we carry around poles and bait cans."

She touched my moustache and the pillow thought returned.

Moving her hand, Susse asked, "What about me?"

I shifted on the hard wooden bench. "We need to know if our hosts are related to the Ravoux who owned the hotel during Vincent's time. If so, they may remember details we won't find in any police reports. You could approach Tania tonight.

"Okay, Mr. Sleuth. What specifically?"

I helped her off the bench. "You might also ask who cleans our rooms and how often. Be nice to know who's going through our belongings while we're away."

"Away fishing?"

Chuckling, we returned to the hotel.

Early the next morning someone knocked on my door. Wrapped in the thin cotton robe I found in the closet, I cracked the door.

Mara, the middle-aged daughter of our host, studied my unshaven face, then glanced at the unbelted robe I wore.

"There's a foreigner here to see you, Mr. Kokk. Shall I bring him up or will you come down?"

"No name?"

She batted translucent eyes. "No name."

"Please send him up," I replied, expecting someone from our embassy.

"By the way, Mara."

A smile flashed as I touched her arm.

"Do you think I could borrow a small radio so I can listen to music up here?"

"I'll ask." She turned and went back down the stairs.

By the time my visitor climbed the stairs, I wore pants and shirt.

"Mr. Kokk? Mr. Jan Kokk?"

"Yes." A young man sporting the beginning of a reddish moustache stood there.

"You are?"

Glancing down the empty hall, he whispered. "Henri Knapper, sir, from the embassy." Silently, he reached into his coat and held up an embossed photo ID.

I motioned him inside and offered him the only chair. I sat on the unmade bed.

"Didn't expect you so soon," I began. "Would you like coffee?"

"No, thank you, sir. I'm instructed to stay here only a minute. To deliver this," again he reached inside his coat and pulled out a Glock pistol, butt first. It was the one I'd selected from Inspector van Groot's table.

"And a holster," he took off his coat and removed a shoulder holster.

"And ammunition," he placed a small box on the bed.

"Thank you," I smiled. "Anything else?"

"Yes, sir. I'm also instructed to advise you that in the event of a *critical* emergency," he repeated 'critical,' "you may call this number." He handed me a slip of yellow paper, "and ask for Daniel.

"I also need your signature on this receipt for the pistol, sir." He extracted a paper, which I signed and returned.

Folding the receipt and placing it in his coat, young Henri Knapper smiled, having accomplished his mission.

He stood and shook my hand. "Goodbye, sir. *Veel geluk.* Good luck."

TWENTY FIVE

"Ready for breakfast?"

Susse answered my knock, nodding. Fully dressed, she stepped out of her room wearing a black sheath and golden earrings.

"Stunning!" I admired her. "We'll have to find you some plain fishing clothing and a big straw hat."

We walked down to the first floor and sat at the same oval dining table as last night. We were alone in the room until Tania Deign bustled in with cups and a pot of coffee.

"Good morning," we repeated her greeting.

She returned before we'd tried the hot coffee with a tray of rolls, cheeses and two large pears.

"Was that a typical French breakfast?" I asked Susse on the way back to our rooms.

"Afraid you'll lose a little weight?" she chided, regarding my middle with amusement.

She unlocked her room and I followed.

Susse stopped and turned, wrinkling her nose. "You're not invited in. Remember our pact?"

Nodding, I began searching her room for hidden listening and recording devices.

About to shriek, she managed "What are you...?"

Shushing her with a finger, I whispered. "I'm searching for listening devices hidden here. I've already covered my room."

She sat on the side of her bed sullenly watching me explore. I looked in all the lighting fixtures, even opened the toilet reservoir. After a hasty search, I found nothing but remained unconvinced that either of our rooms was safe for conversing about our job.

Opening the door between our rooms, I gestured at our worktable.

To my surprise, Mara had already delivered, even installed, a small radio on the table.

I turned the radio to a station playing hip-hop.

Exasperated, Susse moved to the table and punched me with a finger.

"Playing secret agent, Jan? Is this really necessary? I think you've gone overboard."

"Better safe than sorry." I turned the radio louder.

"You claimed to love Beethoven. Now it's hip-hop?"

"The loud music prevents anyone from understanding our conversation when we talk about the case. What did you learn from Tania last night about…"

This time, she interrupted me. "She claims she's the granddaughter of Adeline Ravoux."

I caught my breath. "Great work, Susse. That's excellent. We--rather you--should casually interview Tania a bit more. That makes daughter Mara, Adeline's great granddaughter."

"I thought you'd be interested in Mara." Susse rolled her eyes. "You probably want to interrogate Mara by yourself."

"Who cleans our rooms?" I blinked, disregarding the comment.

"Mara cleans the occupied rooms every day. Don't leave anything about you don't want curious Mara to see."

"You'd better remember that, too. Don't leave that steno pad behind."

Nodding, Susse countered. "What about you? What'd you discover?"

Holding up my pipe, I asked, "Mind if I smoke?"

"I certainly do. Smoke that smelly thing outside somewhere if you insist on parading your masculine bad habits."

No smoking. Instead, I placed the cognac bottle on the table. "Perhaps a bit of VSOP cheer will relax you. Mara's name seems to anger you. By the way," I leaned forward, conspiratorially. "Mara must be all of fifty years old. Maybe more."

Susse stared at the cognac. "So early in the day, Jan? Is this how you began all those investigations for which you are reputedly famous?"

I poured a jigger of the golden liquor before answering the question. "We must apply for the fishing licenses at the office of *le maire*, if that's how you say 'mayor.'

"Luckily," I continued, "there is a used clothing and furniture shop just down the street. Maybe we'll find something suitable for fishing. The poles, tackle and bait are all available at a fishing stand on the river somewhere near the church."

Concluding, I suggested we acquire the licenses, clothing and gear this morning. "Wouldn't fishing enthusiasts spend the rest of the day on the river?"

"I thought we were here to investigate. Not smoke, drink," she eyed the jigger of cognac, "fish or encourage fifty-year old maids?"

"You'll look ravishing in a simple fishing frock and straw hat, dear Susse."

"Don't say that!" she muttered. "I'm *not* your 'Dear Anything!'"

To prove her point, she grabbed the jigger and downed it in one gulp.

Three hours later, we were duly licensed and attired for sport. We put on the hand-me-downs purchased from the local thrift shop, then filed downstairs. The luncheon menu was hearty omelets, more cheese and red wine.

As Mara cleared the table, she bent down over me. "Is the radio satisfactory?"

"Fine, Mara, fine. I appreciate all you're doing."

She smiled. "Anything you need, please tell me." With a stoic look at Susse, Mara bounced back into the kitchen.

I must have watched the movement appreciatively.

Susse slammed down her wineglass, almost breaking it. "I'm to sit here, watching you cozy up to that, that cougar?

"Plus translate her words of endearment? You're disgusting, Mr. Kokk!"

'Disgusting' was the same word she later used as I baited her fishing hook with a silvery minnow on the banks of the Oise River.

She waved away the fly attracted by the bait. "I can't do this more than once," she warned. "Then I'll stay in my room until we return to Paris."

"Sophie won't be there for another week or two," I argued, holding her pole. "Let me show you how to cast."

Our selected fishing spot was deserted. "This is a good place for us to talk about our work.

"Among the questions we must answer are these: where's the pistol with which Vincent was shot? Another, what happened to all his painting paraphernalia--the canvas, paints, brushes and easel--he carried with him that afternoon?"

Susse seemed interested for the first time. "Point taken. Only the murderer--if it was murder--would have dumped those things somewhere. Find them, determine who last had them and we have solved the case."

Casting my line as far into the stream as possible, I spat. "Even if those items could be found, what could they reveal after so long a time?"

She was adamant. "Whoever turned them in or kept them is the culprit."

Pointing to the river, I shrugged. "The river offers the easiest place to dispose of the pistol. If it's out there," I pointed, "it's under twenty feet or more of sediment and muck. No wonder the police couldn't find it."

She gave her pole an excited tug. "Jan, I think something's trying to take my bait!"

"Relax. Let him."

"Why does it always have to be a 'him'?" She peered over her shoulder at me, making a face.

"There it is again!"

"Relax," I repeated. By the bend of the pole, she had snagged something. Maybe a weed.

"If you still feel something's there, walk straight back with your pole in the air until the hook is out of the water."

She licked her lips. "Did the police even try?" She pulled the line taunt and started edging backward.

Dropping my own fishing pole, I stepped next to her.

She hissed "Stay away! This is my fish!"

Pleased by her sudden addiction to fishing, I stopped. "Did the police try what?"

"Try diving in the river for the pistol of course!

"Damn! I think I just lost him!"

Later, sitting on a bench overlooking our fishing spot we reviewed tidbits about the case.

"It would be great if you continue small talk with Tania."

"Woman's work, eh, Jan? What do you want me to smooth talk her about?"

"Let's start after supper tonight. Invite her to share a glass or two of wine."

"What's my assignment, Mr. Sleuth?"

"I wish you would call me Jan."

"You insultingly refer to me as 'Professor' What's the difference, Mister?"

I tamped-out my pipe. "Sorry. Didn't know the word offended. I apologize."

Clearing my throat, I charged ahead.

"Let's develop a friendly relationship with that lady. For example, we should learn as much as possible about her grandmother, her memories of famous guests, who were her favorites, history of the hotel, things like that."

"Where would you hide a pistol used in a shooting?" she mused. "I guess the painting materials Vincent carried were destroyed or discarded long ago."

Susse suddenly turned on the bench. "What will you be doing while I sit in the dining room noodling Tania? Interrogating the spinster daughter upstairs in your room?"

"Not at all," I demurred. "Maurice and I have yet to talk about another important person in this mystery."

"Who?"

"Van Gogh's local physician and friend, of course. Doctor Gachet. Like Vincent, he suffered a similar malady.

"While you chat-up the wife, I'll share a few drinks with the husband. Maybe he'll introduce us to the Gachets, if there are still Gachet descendants living here."

"If the sleuth would like my advice…"

I interrupted. "You promised not to call me that."

She bobbed her head. "Right. My turn to apologize. Would you like to hear the advice anyway?"

"Absolutely."

"Beware of that spinster daughter. I can tell she'd like nothing better than stalk and strip search you."

I winked. "Since your room and mine-—even our beds--—are side-by-side, separated by a thin wall, I expect you to rush to my rescue."

The loose door glass rattled as Lieutenant Fouranger knocked then entered the office of his captain.

Captain Coffier swore. He'd written a long work order explaining why the door should be replaced. Where was that new door?

"They have arrived in Paris, Captain."

Coffier folded his morning newspaper. "Who?"

"The investigator from the Netherlands, sir." The lieutenant frowned. "We talked about him just yesterday and you said…"

"I know very well what I said, Lieutenant," Coffier snapped. "This is today, bring me up to speed."

"The big man and a female arrived from Amsterdam and are probably on their way, maybe even in the village by now." He checked his watch.

"You told me to establish surveillance as discreetly as possible."

"Yes, yes. What was their destination?"

Fourange wondered if his superior had been drinking this early. "Auvers-sur-Oise, Captain. They're at the village to investigate the death of that crazy Dutch painter."

"Yes, yes. Of course," Couffier stood up to stare out his window. Not all offices boasted of a window this large. This one was dirty. He made a mental note to send a work order to have it cleaned. Immediately.

"Very well, Lieutenant. Carry on. Keep up the good work. I depend on you to keep me posted on that situation."

"Very good, sir." Lieutenant Fourange smiled as he closed the door just hard enough to rattle the glass.

TWENTY SIX

At breakfast the next morning, an absorbed Susse peered absently at me as I sat across from her at a small table.

"How are you today?"

My greeting didn't register.

"Wait 'til you hear," she said, briskly stirring her coffee, "what I discovered."

"Later," she answered my look. "Upstairs? Or is fishing on the agenda this morning?"

Her glee was contagious. "You choose," I replied as Tania presented eggs, sausage and thick bread.

The couple named Schenk from Alsace-Lorraine, still wearing dusty black, looked away when we later stood to leave. Their sudden movement made me suspect they'd heard every word we had said while we ate breakfast.

Upstairs, I opened Susse's door for her, then the door dividing our rooms. We sat at our makeshift work desk and I turned on the radio borrowed from Mara.

Susse opened her steno pad and began reading from it, glancing up after every paragraph for a reaction.

"Tania and I are chums already," she gestured. "We had a long talk last night which cost you two bottles of good burgundy. That's her favorite."

Not wanting to slow down her narrative, I just nodded.

"Her stories about Adeline, her grandmother, were fascinating. Tania claims Adeline had a schoolgirl crush on their famous painter-lodger."

"Vincent?"

"Who else? Her father was furious when he heard Adeline had been up in Vincent's garret room. According to Tania, his rage at Vincent became more violent due to that incident. He even demanded Vincent's rent in advance.

"Adeline admired all the painters who had lived in their hotel but Vincent was her favorite. He asked her to pose as his model for the painting you saw in the museum."

She held a finger to her lips. "It all went well except for…"

"What?"

"You've infected me with your secrecy. That young man we met at supper the first night was seated near Tania and myself. Although he pretended to read a magazine, I think he was listening to our every word."

"You mean the one writing a dissertation about the old church?"

"Yes. Louis something."

"He said his name was Louis Monoud. Thank you for your alertness and all this useful information."

Exuberant, I leaned forward and bused her on the cheek. "Excellent job! Now we have a glimmer of motive."

Expecting a slap or punch, I quickly sat back. "Where are you keeping your notepad?"

"Like I told you, under my pillow at night. It's with me at all other times."

Apparently forgiving the spontaneous kiss, she opened her notebook. "Now tell me what you discovered."

"Not as much as you but we have an appointment this afternoon with a member of the Gachet family, thanks to Maurice.

"Maurice was most cordial after we shared a few drinks in the bar. Can you imagine? The Gachets still live in the old doctor's house on Rue Remy, not far from here. I hope to…."

"*We* hope to," she tapped my palm. "*We* hope to find more clues."

She stood and stretched. "Meanwhile, let's go fishing. I'm going to catch the big one that got away yesterday."

Maurice, our host and my drinking partner, told me where the deepest part of the river was, thus the best fishing. Today we switched from minnows to worms. Susse shut her eyes, I baited a hook and threw her line into the water.

"This is supposed to be the deepest section of the river near Auvers," I said, watching her cast.

She bit a lip as she cast again, farther. "Then this is where that pistol may have been tossed."

While baiting my hook I looked around the surrounding trees and hedges. A small gray auto was parked, partially hidden, behind a windrow and thicket some distance away.

Expecting a game warden checking fishing licenses, I opened my canvas handbag.

"Jan!" Her cry erased my interest in the gray car.

She was at the edge of the deep river, being pulled into the water by something on her line.

I grabbed her waist and reached for the pole. Jerked from her hands, it was in the water and moving away in spurts.

I splashed into the river, seizing the butt of the pole. The pull was strong enough that I fell to my knees in the water before stopping the pole and line.

I slipped several times getting back on the riverbank where Susse stood aghast.

Lifting the pole as far as I could we saw what had taken the bait, almost her line and pole, too.

Susse squealed in pleasure. "It's a monster! I caught a monster!" She kept yelling while pounding my wet back.

On the bank, the monster became a nice ten-inch shad. I picked it up by the gills and offered it to her.

Ignoring the fish, she clutched my arm. "Oh, Jan. You're completely soaked and cold! We've got to get you back to the hotel and into dry clothes."

Gathering up the bait can and poles I asked "What about your monster fish?" I dangled it in front of her.

"Throw it back! It's dirty and slimy!"

When I hesitated to toss the shad into the river, she commanded "Do it!"

Inwardly beaming that I--not the fish--held her attention, we returned to the hotel. I changed clothing and joined her in the dining room.

TWENTY SEVEN

As we approached the Gachet residence on Rue Remy, Susse grabbed my arm. "Oh, Jan! Look at that!"

She pointed at an old-fashioned weathered house with a discolored turret and garden, comfortable but unassuming. Susse thought otherwise.

"Oh, it's just like Cezanne's painting of this house in the 1870's!"

She giggled at my expression. "That painting hangs in our museum. No," she shook her head, "you didn't see it since we were concentrating on the van Goghs."

The wood-crossed door opened after we knocked and an elderly man wearing a hunting jacket and flannels greeted us.

"Come in, come in," he gestured. "You are exactly on time for afternoon coffee." He pointed toward the parlor.

"I'm Robert Gachet and welcome you in the name of my great uncle, the eminent physician, to his former--my present--home."

Susse and I introduced ourselves: she did so smoothly while I stumbled with my few French words. "It is most kind of you to see us, Mr. Gachet."

He indicated a large sofa in the parlor where a tray with cups and saucers waited on a side table.

After a few pleasantries I reiterated the reason for our visit. "We are attempting to reconstruct the last days of Vincent van Gogh's life. Our efforts would be meaningless without including the contributions of his great friend, physician and adviser, Doctor Paul Gachet, your great uncle."

Robert Gachet nodded approvingly either at my words or at his housekeeper serving the coffee. Peering at us, he interlaced his fingers. "Maurice Deign called me about your visit. He said you are with the van Gogh Museum, Ms. Thankker?"

"Yes, sir. I am the curator there." She smiled at my surprise at her title.

Gachet turned to me. "You, Mr. Kokk. Are you also with that famous museum?"

"No. Mr. Gachet. I'm here representing the Dutch Ministry of Arts."

Apparently satisfied with our replies, Gachet tapped his cup. "How may I help?"

Susse beamed. "We have access to the several official reports about van Gogh's demise but they neglect the personal and professional relationship provided the painter by your great uncle.

"Those official reports, although voluminous, neglect or overlook Doctor Gachet's tremendous influence on his friend and patient."

As we'd discussed, I added. "As well as the painter's devotion and personal admiration of his physician. We hope to rectify that."

Robert Gachet eyed us, nodding. We lapsed into silence, sipping coffee.

Finally he spoke. "For years our family has felt as you do. But how does one 'rectify' an old, but hurtful oversight?"

My turn again. "By discovering material--documents, diaries, notes and such--which the police overlooked in their haste to close a tragic incident."

Solemnly, Susse watched Gachet. "We appeal to you for any advice or assistance you might offer our research."

She lowered her voice. "To rectify history for the whole world."

Abruptly Gachet rose from his chair and began pacing. "Please forgive my manners. If I sit too long, the knees complain."

He walked to a small window overlooking the garden, turned and limped back. Thinking this was his signal to excuse ourselves we stood and thanked him for his time.

He gestured toward the upstairs. "I must discuss your request with my family. I'm certain you're aware of not only our pride in our illustrious ancestor but our sensitivity and caution.

"I'll contact you tomorrow with our decision. You remain at the Hotel Ravoux?"

After dinner downstairs, Susse and I returned to our rooms. I opened her door and she motioned me in, accepting my presence without the usual warning. I opened the common door and we sat around the worktable. I turned up the little radio's volume.

Reaching into my satchel, I extracted the cognac. Taking two clean glasses from the bath, I poured drinks.

"Your health, Ms. Thankker. You did exceedingly well today."

She accepted the glass and toast. After a sip, she tabled the glass. "I don't normally drink this terrible stuff but a sip may cheer me."

"You miss Sophie of course."

Susse closed her eyes a moment before answering. "Yes I do. I must admit, though, you temporarily have diverted me with fishing. Never tried it before."

She took another, longer sip. "I don't feel we've made any progress in this investigation, Jan. Still think we can be back in Amsterdam within two weeks?"

I held up my pipe for approval. To my surprise, she didn't object. Praise and credit the cognac, I thought.

"We're doing fine," I packed the pipe.

"Investigations begin slowly. We never initially know where to find the passion usually accompanying murder.

"If we get good news from Gachet tomorrow, we may know where to find that passion."

I lit the pipe with a kitchen match, inhaled, and then gambled with a personal question. "Have you always felt that way about women?"

Susse sniffed, either at the tobacco or my audacity. "Although, it's none of your business, the answer is 'no,' I've not always felt 'that way,' as you quaintly put it."

She ran a hand through her tousled hair. "You've been a gentleman and I appreciate that. You even jumped into the river for me today."

She offered her glass. "I hope I don't regret this conversation."

I refilled the glasses. "We're colleagues and--I hope—good, lasting friends."

She lifted the canvas bag I'd dropped on the floor after our river excursion. "What's in this? Why so heavy?"

"Just my passport, penknife and a camera," I lied, thinking it better not to tell her about the pistol.

She finished her drink and arose to go to her room.

"*A bientot,*" I tried my French.

Hand on the knob, she turned. "Good night, Jan. Thank you for the cognac and companionship. Don't go overboard as you did in the river, thinking my door is unlocked."

She grinned. "It isn't!"

TWENTY EIGHT

My hall door opened at 6:30 that morning. Groggily, I sat up in the warm bed, reaching under my pillow for the pistol.

Daughter Mara stood there, balancing a surprise breakfast tray. "I thought you deserved breakfast in bed," she began, nudging me over on the bed with the tray in her lap.

She handed me a cup of coffee. "My, you're a handsome man this time of morning," she began, filling the other cup for herself.

She scoffed at my surprise. "Thought it past time we got to know each other better."

Next she offered me a small plate of buttered scones.

"You're certainly a surprise, Mara," I managed, trying to sit up. "I shall always remember this example of Ravoux hospitality." I picked out two scones.

She stood and pulled off her apron. "Perhaps you'd like a different sample of Ravoux hospitality?"

She lifted the bed linens. "Scoot over."

By that time I was out the other side of the bed and pulling up my trousers. "No, Mara. Maybe next time."

Hearing the response, I couldn't believe it came from me.

Offering a hasty alibi, I said "We would wake up my next-door neighbor."

"So that's the way it is, is it? That *Hollandais* slip of a woman is your mistress?"

She emptied the cups, slamming them on the tray. "Thought you'd prefer a mature, full-bodied companion.

"Like me!" She replaced the dish on the tray and kicked the door shut on her way out.

By the time I reached the dining room, Susse was seated with Tania and Louis, the lodger writing a dissertation. Seeing me approach, Louis scowled and scurried out the door.

"Welcome, Jan," Susse gaily greeted me. Her eyes had a glint I'd not seen before.

"Just coffee, Tania," I asked as she started for the kitchen.

"Not hungry, Jan? Even after that early morning exertion I heard from your room?"

"You must realize the walls here are very thin," she smirked.

Wearing an innocent face, I retorted. "You're mistaken about the 'exertion,' as you put it. There was none of that. I escaped as soon as courtesy permitted."

I debated telling Susse the details but instead stirred the coffee.

Nodding in the direction Louis Monoud had taken, I asked. "What was his rush?"

She tittered. "You're jealous?"

"Of course not," I blustered. "Have I reason to be?"

Unable to retract the question, I followed with a snappy "What'd he want?"

She drew her chair closer. "Tania says he asks lots of questions about you. Me, too."

"Well, he's obviously smitten with you, glamorous Susse. Who wouldn't be?"

She caught her breath. "You *are* jealous!"

Tania returned to our table and looked at Susse. "There's a telephone call for you at the desk."

As Susse left, I smacked my lips. "Coffee's excellent, Tania. Where's Mara this morning?"

She shrugged. "Upstairs making beds, I guess."

"How's Louis Monoud's writing, research--or whatever--going? Did he say?"

"No," she rolled her eyes. "I think he's more interested in your friend."

I leaned forward to pour more coffee from the pot. "Does he have an automobile?"

She nodded. "Yes, I see it every morning in our parking area."

"Is it a small, gray one? Maybe a Peugeot?"

Tania's answer was obliterated by an exuberant Susse returning from the telephone.

"Good news! Gachet will see us at eleven!"

Apprehensively, we knocked on the same thick old wooden door at exactly eleven. I returned the gold pocket watch to my vest as the door opened. The old watch's audible ticking encouraged me that this second visit would be productive.

Gachet opened the door, shook our hands and indicated the sofa we'd occupied the day before.

"Thank you again for seeing us, sir," Susse began. "I appreciate your telephone call this morning and invitation to hear your family's decision."

Gachet eyed us as carefully as before, then rang a small bell for the housekeeper. "Coffee, or is it too late for you? Perhaps a glass of our excellent Val d'Oise wine?"

Thinking the offer was intended to soften our disappointment at what he'd next say, we hesitated.

I answered after a moment. "Coffee would be fine." Refusing hospitality was probably considered rude in tiny Auvers.

As coffee was served, we made the usual conversation about the weather, the river and finally, fishing.

"Ms. Thankker is fond of fishing," I volunteered. "We were at the river just yesterday."

He looked surprised. "Did you catch any thing?"

Blushing, Susse held out her hands to show the size of the shad. "I returned it to the river. With luck I'll hook a bigger one today."

Joining long fingers, he smiled. "Perhaps I am adding to your luck. My family has agreed to offer you portions of a document which you may find helpful in your research."

We caught our breath. In unison, we responded "Wonderful!"

"However there are strict conditions to your use of this document. For example, it cannot be removed from our home."

Susse and I looked at each other, nodding.

"We also must approve any portion of your report that mentions our ancestor.

"Do you understood and agree with them without reservation?"

Susse looked at me. After a moment, I found words. "Your first condition about removing the document is agreeable. We'll simply photograph copies if you'll permit that."

Susse couldn't contain her question. "What is the document?"

"It is our ancient family Bible," he announced with pride. "Several pages are filled with Doctor Gachet's handwritten recollection of events leading to and after van Gogh's passing."

She was jubilant. "Amazing! At the time did the police examine those recollections?"

"No. Definitely not." His answer was quick. "They didn't ask for any documents, I'm told, nor was it offered since it is our family Bible."

I leaned back in the sofa, fearing his reaction to my careful words.

"Mr. Gachet, the second condition may pose a problem. The Ministry of Arts of our government is highly appreciative of your assistance and intends to thank you in an appropriate manner. It will be pleased to provide you an advance copy of its final published report.

"However, I doubt the Ministry would allow editing or changing their official document.

"Could your family reconsider the second condition providing an advance copy of the report is made available to you?"

Closing his eyes, he rubbed his forehead. "I'll present my family with your objections and alternative."

His tone changed. "Until then I wish you both a good day."

"Our chances of seeing the Gachet 'recollections' seem to be fading," she moaned as we walked back to the hotel. I agreed. Gachet's manner suggested that his family's answer would be a resounding 'no.'

Our innkeeper greeted us as we entered the hotel. Wild-eyed, Maurice Deign stood there staring at us and wringing his hands. His wife and daughter warily stood behind him, their faces taunt and anxious.

He exploded once we were inside.

"It is terrible! Terrible! Such a thing has never occurred before at the *Auberge Ravoux.*"

Rasping with emotion, he pumped my hand while apologizing about something in rapid French.

"What's he saying, Susse?"

"Your poor car, Monsieur! Tania noticed it this morning when she went for the mail. I called the police immediately. I am so sorry! Never! Never before!"

His staccato French was too fast. I turned again to Susse.

"Our car tires have been slashed!"

TWENTY NINE

Before going to our rooms, Susse and I used the reception telephone to call the auto rental agency in Paris. She explained our dilemma and asked for replacement tires or another vehicle.

Still muttering, Maurice himself delivered a complimentary bottle of *cabernet sauvignon* to our rooms. As he left, I turned up the radio on the worktable.

"It will be tomorrow or later before the car is repaired or replaced, Jan. What do we do now?"

"I'd hoped we could tour the various sites rumored to be where the murder...ah...shooting took place.

"Instead, let's go over these old statements again. We can't just sit around waiting on the Gachets or a new vehicle."

I passed her a folder. "Here are several statements from Adeline, Gustave Ravoux's thirteen-year old daughter. That makes her Tania's grandmother, right?"

"Right." Susse looked up from her steno pad. "Tell me, Jan. You are convinced that Vincent was murdered, right? Convince me."

Without asking, I tamped and lit my pipe. "What was the point of that excellent instruction you gave me at the museum about his paintings? Wasn't it your thesis that van Gogh--although flawed--was too enthused about sunflowers, wheat fields and sleepy villages to be suicidal?"

She opened a window to let the smoke out. "*D'accord*, Jan. You said a requirement of murder is passion, thus motive. Where are they?"

Delaying, I asked. "Now you're teaching me French?"

Susse winked. "Won't Mara go crazy from your endearments in French instead of Dutch?"

"Not funny, Susse. I was about to commend you for the feedback you've gained today. You are a good investigator. I may offer you a position after this."

She stamped her foot. "There you go, dreaming again. Stop it!"

Contentedly puffing on the pipe I continued. "Example: you found out that Adeline had a school girl crush on van Gogh making her father, Gustave, furious at his lodger. That's both passion and motive."

She sat down heavily. "Alright, now let's look for others. Here's Adeline speaking in 1956 about the location of the shooting. I'm quoting:

Vincent had gone toward the wheat field where he had painted before. In the deep path that runs along the wall of the chateau sitting in front of the cemetery and wheat field--as my father understood it--Vincent shot himself.

"Notice she's repeating what her father told her. Ring a bell for Gustave Ravoux's missing motive. He did it himself!"

"Who says she was telling the truth?" I objected.

"Why would she lie?"

"Young girl, smitten with the admiring lodger living upstairs in her family's inn. Vincent even painted Adeline's portrait which you showed me at the museum." I blew a near-perfect smoke ring.

"I wonder how her father felt about her sitting alone with Vincent for a portrait?" Susse mused.

"He probably raised the roof about it," I guessed. "That's why she refused a second sitting with Vincent to finish that portrait."

Susse blinked her eyes. "You have yet to understand women, Jan. It's so simple.

"Vincent didn't share the teenager's feelings and told her so. Of course she refused to sit for him again. She'd been rejected. It wasn't because of her father."

Defensively, I parried. "Did you forget about London?"

"What about London?"

"In London Vincent fell in love with the daughter of his landlady, you said. Perhaps Vincent similarly fell in love with the daughter of his Auvers landlord." I blew another smoke ring.

Susse made a face. "I agree he was a romantic. Why would a thirty--almost forty--year old fall in love with Adeline, only thirteen?

"Really, Jan!"

"Time for lunch," I announced rather than concede. "We can't leave our folders and notes laying about up here."

"Problem solved," Susse scooped the papers together and stuffed them into my canvas handbag.

"Your bag is certainly heavy," she peered into it before I could stop her.

"Looks like a pistol down there. When were you going to tell me about that?"

THIRTY

We were alone in the dining room except for Tania, waiting on us. Mara winked at me each time she walked by our table.

Between bites of mushroom omelet, Susse upbraided me. "Really, Jan. You shouldn't encourage that woman. I heard her through the wall this morning."

Spreading my hands, I again declared my innocence. Maurice rushed into the dining room and stopped.

"Sorry to disturb you, sir."

"Good day, Maurice. What is it?"

"The police, sir. They're in the parking area searching your car!"

I folded my napkin and stood. Simultaneously Susse and I frowned at the canvas handbag at my feet. We had the same thought.

She stood and grabbed the bag, whispering "I'll take care of it."

Glancing at Mara standing by the kitchen door, Susse leaned over and kissed my cheek. Tania giggled at the look on my face.

"See you soon, darling!" Susse playfully added in my ear, loud enough for Mara to hear.

Glowering, Mara wrinkled her nose at Susse before storming out, slamming the kitchen door.

Once the police left, I knocked on Susse's door. She unlocked it.

"Quick thinking on your part about my canvas bag! Thanks, Susse! The police would have searched that little bag had I been carrying it.

"You saved me a night, or longer, in the local lock-up, trying to explain the pistol."

Absently, she nodded, studying some papers. She motioned me to join her at the worktable. She turned up the radio volume in case of eavesdroppers.

I remembered Susse's dining room tease. "I'm back, darling, and ready to resume where we stopped in the dining room."

Susse chortled. "What do they say in those American movies? 'Only in your dreams!'"

"Behave and sit down," she admonished. "Let's explore Adeline Ravoux's statements again. She talked a lot to different interrogators. Some of what she told them was contradictory.

"Here's an example. In a 1960 interview, she claimed that the pistol with which Vincent was shot belonged to her father. Vincent borrowed it from her father that fatal Sunday, she said, to 'scare away crows.'

"That reinforced the legend that his shooting took place where he painted 'Wheat Field with Crows.'"

I chimed in. "From other reports, it appears a farm yard west of the village was the real site of the shooting.

"We have statements here from two different elderly ladies who lived in Auvers. One said:

Van Gogh left the Ravoux Inn in the direction of Chaponval, a small hamlet west of Auvers. At the Rue Boucher he entered a small farmyard. There he hid behind a large manure pile. There he committed the act that led to his death…

Susse read from the second statement.

My grandfather saw Vincent leave the Ravoux Inn that day and walk in the direction of Chaponval.

"Also this lady's grandfather watched van Gogh enter a small farmyard on the Rue Boucher. Then he heard a gunshot but didn't investigate. He was probably frightened."

"Damn shame," I shook my head. "Had he gone into that farmyard, we might have a real witness statement.

"Very peculiar, wasn't it that the grandfather backed off instead of investigating the gunshot?"

"Yes," she agreed. "The farmyard was only a half-mile *west* of the Ravoux Inn. That fabled wheat field mentioned by Adeline was *east*, on the other side of Auvers. These two reports tell us the actual location of the shooting.

"True...." She pointed a finger at me. "Back to that famous missing pistol.

"Why did Adeline not mention the pistol in her interview? Wouldn't it have been among the first questions asked by the police?"

I repacked the pipe. "Simple. The young girl was trying to protect her father from suspicion."

Susse raised two fingers. "You just rang the bell again supporting a motive for innkeeper Gustave Ravoux."

"Or a motive for Adeline Ravoux herself?" As I spoke, I doubted it.

To reinforce the idea, I said "See, our smitten young girl followed Vincent to his painting spot after lunch that Sunday. She intended to confess her love for him or to accuse him of perfidy.

"The exchange between them became heated. She snatched the old pistol from Vincent, shot him and--terrified about what she'd done--ran home to hide."

"Nonsense, Jan. She wasn't strong enough to lift that heavy pistol, much less to aim and pull a clumsy trigger."

"How do you know it was heavy? The pistol was never found."

"Nor were his painting supplies which he carried from the hotel that day," she added. "We have a lot to learn. Those Gachet recollections might provide some answers."

I poured and we raised a toast to our extraordinary acuity as investigators.

Taking a break, we went to the parking area to look at our car and its mutilated tires.

She was first to voice it. "Who could have done such a thing?"

"Well," I teased, "you highly irritated lovely Mara today."

"The tires were slashed last night, Jan. A woman would never resort to that. It had to be a vengeful male."

I ticked off a finger. "Not Maurice, our host. He appeared genuinely upset."

"Unless our host is a remarkable actor," she quibbled. "Perhaps it was the dissertation writer. What's his name?"

"You know his name," I kidded. "He's stalking you. He knifed the tires to keep you here indefinitely until he wins your heart."

"All men are ridiculous," she snapped. "You know my preference."

"Yes but Louis Monard doesn't. Unless you told him last night?"

Shoving, she took the car keys from me and opened the doors. "Let's walk our poles and tackle to the river. I need some fishing and fresh air."

THIRTY ONE

We sat on the bench watching the lines and floats bob in the currents of the Oise. The sounds of the river were soothing, subduing conversation.

Finally Susse broke the spell. "You claimed my comments at the museum supported my 'thesis' that Vincent was not suicidal."

"Did I say 'thesis?'"

"You did. Now," she challenged, "I want to hear why you think it was *not* suicide."

Packing the pipe gave me time to ready a reply. "I admire the way we work together, like this." I lit the pipe, further delaying an answer.

"Skip the banter, Jan. Get to the crux."

"First, if you decided to shoot yourself, where would you aim?"

She looked impish. "You haven't driven me that far yet."

"I suppose I'd aim for the heart."

"Exactly. Vincent's wound was in the lower abdomen, neither heart nor head. I'm no doctor but a wound there sounds quite painful.

"The angle of the entry wound seemed odd to the two doctors attending Vincent. Entry was at an angle to the abdomen, not perpendicular. I'd bet most suicide gun wounds are straight into the torso, not oblique.

"Gun powder residue may have been unrecognized in those days but the doctors also mentioned that the bullet must have been fired 'from too far out' for Vincent to have pulled the trigger.

"Another oddity, don't you think?"

Eyes closed, she leaned back on the bench, forehead wrinkled in concentration.

"*D'accord.*" She opened her eyes. "Okay. Anything else?"

Pleased with a smoke ring, I continued. "Yes, there's the absence of a suicide letter or note. Vincent's older brother, Theo, found none after searching Vincent's room.

"Wouldn't you have written a final goodbye to Sophie?"

"Stop it, Jan! Don't say her name! That's rude and morose."

"You asked. I have more questions."

Biting her lip she giggled. "Shoot."

"Why did Vincent take his canvases, easel, paints, brushes and other materials with him that afternoon if he intended to kill himself?"

"Point taken," she admitted.

"One last question. Days before the shooting, Vincent placed a large order for more paints. Why would he have ordered more expensive paints if he was going to shoot himself on Sunday?"

Susse rushed to her fishing pole stuck in the earth. It was being pulled into the water.

"A bite! A bite!" She jumped into the water fully clothed in pursuit of the pole.

Seeing her caught by the strong current, I followed, grabbing and pulling her out. We were both drenched.

After a warm bath and dry clothes, Susse allowed me to pour her another small tot of cognac.

"To counteract possible fever and cold," I lifted my glass. "*Proost!*"

Blonde hair hidden in the wrapped towel, she blinked before joining the toast. "You can be quite the gentleman on occasion, I've decided."

"Oh?"

"You've come to my rescue and pulled me out of the river twice now. You bear close watching, Sir Gallahad."

"Just another 'tricky male' you called me in Amsterdam," I jousted.

She pushed her glass to me for a refill. "I sincerely thank you, Jan Kokk, for saving me from the river. You are a rarity among your species."

"Thank you. Feel up to supper?"

She tipped her glass. "Think I'd rather have something light-- sandwiches, maybe--up here. How about you?"

"Sounds good."

She held her glass up to the light, admiring the color of the cognac. "This stuff certainly warms me.

"Before you go down and order sandwiches for two, I have a request."

"Tell me."

"That your Mara not deliver them."

After the sandwiches, she yawned and bid me good night. Susse closed the door between our rooms. I heard the lock snap.

At the same moment, there was a knock on my other door. Guessing it was inquisitive Mara, I called out "C'mon in."

She stood in the door wearing a tight dark dress, balancing a tray in one hand. "Help me with this, Jan," she gushed, entering sideways with the tray.

"I heard Dutchmen like their beer before bedtime. Snacks, too."

She gestured at tiny sausages and cheese as she set the tray on the worktable. Glancing at the closed door to Susse's room, she smoothed her skirt. "Now isn't this cozy, just the two of us."

The bottles were frosty Grolsch Dutch lager. I couldn't refuse such hospitality and held the chair for her. Perhaps she bore a message as well as the Grolsch?

"You're working late, Mara. Have all your guests gone to bed?"

Mara popped the flip-tops and handed me one. She sat, looking about the room. "No photos of wife and family?"

"None," I admitted.

Looking at the folders still on the worktable, she asked, "What's all this? Are you writing a story about the old church like young Louis?"

I tasted the Grolsch, as happy with the topic she'd just opened as the lager. "How's his writing coming? Have you read it?"

I gestured at the folders. "Does he work in his room, like me?"

"Yeah, he writes on a laptop but I haven't read anything of his. What are you and her," she inclined her head toward Susse's room, "writing about?"

"We're really here for the fishing. My friend is a commercial photographer. She's taking her photos of the river and countryside back to Amsterdam for a showing next month.

"That's how we finance our fishing and travels."

She swallowed a mouthful of lager. "I'd like to see some of her pics."

"Me, too. Her film is a special type that can't be developed locally. Requires equipment she designed in Amsterdam."

Mara puckered her lips. "You two are just business friends, then?" With that she edged off the chair and onto the bed.

"We're friends as well as business associates." I gulped the rest of the beer and set it on the tray.

"Speaking of work, we have an early appointment in the morning," I lied, stretching and yawning.

"Need to get some rest. Nice of you to drop by, Mara."

Her face contorted. "Don't expect any more favors--or midnight visits--from me!" she screeched.

I locked the door after her.

THIRTY TWO

There was no answer when I tapped on Susse's door the next morning so I walked down to the dining room. She sat at a corner table with Louis Monoud. Based on Mara's remarks, I could ask likely questions about his work at the church of Auvers.

"*Bon jour,*" I greeted them in my best French and sat down opposite Louis.

"Mara's been telling me about your interesting work at the *Place de l'Eglise.*"

"Pardon?" His startled look meant he didn't recognize the street address of the famous church he claimed to be researching.

I helped with a hint. "Your dissertation, how's it coming along? Will you be submitting it soon?"

Susse raised an eyebrow at me. My attention remained on Louis. "You must be studying at the Val d'Oise University?"

"Yes. Yes, I am. The paper's going very well, thank you. I hope to submit it to my professor by Christmas. If he accepts it, then I'll defend it before the doctoral committees.

"If you both will excuse me," he smiled with relief. "I have an early appointment to study the church altar fixtures."

Smiling, he intoned an aside to Susse, "Hope to see you later."

I signaled Tania for coffee and baguettes. "Didn't mean to intrude," I studied Susse. What had she and Louis been talking about so earnestly?"

She slapped me on the back. "Of course you did! You've wanted to question him since we arrived. What's your impression?"

"Of our so-called scholar or of your radiant appearance?"

She punched me on the shoulder. "Jan Kokk, gifted early morning male sweet-talker!"

She lowered her voice. "Seriously, he questioned what we're doing here. I told him we were vacationing and fishing."

"So we can fabricate in tandem," I leaned forward. "I told Mara we were here fishing and that you are a professional photographer."

"I heard most of that through the wall," she joked. "I'm proud of you, Jan! You didn't take advantage of fat Mara's attempt to throw herself on your mercy--or was it on your bed?"

We were silent as Tania served coffee and baguettes. Susse spoke first. "I hope the car is repaired or replaced today."

Wiping spilled coffee, I agreed. "Me, too. I'd like to hear from the noble Gachet family today. Our investigation is stagnant! We need more information and soon."

After coffee, we returned to our rooms and I reached for the radio. Accidentally, I edged it off the table and it fell on the floor. As I picked it up, the radio's cardboard back panel came off.

I held a finger to my lips and grabbed a pad and pencil. "Don't speak," I wrote, holding the note up to her eyes.

Then I wrote "This little item." I pointed with the pencil to the back of the radio, "looks like a transmitter. Someone's been hearing or recording what we say in here."

Susse studied it, nodding understanding. "Let's grab our poles and go fishing," she announced aloud. "Our vacation ends soon and I want to land another big shad today."

"That's exactly what we're here for," I agreed, carefully replacing the radio's back panel.

After baiting hooks and sticking the poles into the earth, we sat on the bench, watching the currents flow. The Oise seemed faster today than when I pulled Susse out of the water yesterday.

She seemed clairvoyant. "You're thinking about your rescuing me from drowning."

"No," I fibbed. "My mind was on how appealing you looked in wet, clinging clothing."

She blushed. "Enough of that! Tell me what will we do about that listening device in the radio? Wouldn't turning the radio volume on loud keep listeners from understanding what we say?"

"Partially," I admitted. "Here's an idea: we use it to our advantage, deceiving the listeners whoever, wherever they are.

"We intentionally feed them lies. If we previously said, as we did, 'Ravoux had a motive' now we announce that we were mistaken."

Her eyes sparkled. "That we are at a loss to determine any motive, to confuse our unknown bad guys?"

"Exactly. You'll make a great investigator, Susse. All you need is more practice working with an experienced investigator somewhere in the lovely, warm Caribbean.

"Like me!

"Like Curacao!"

Her expressive eyes widened, either in fright or in surprise at my proposal.

She turned to watch the fishing lines. "Who are those listeners, Jan?"

"Probably the same people who are driving away in that little gray auto." I pointed at the departing vehicle. It had parked nearby behind bramble bushes and trees as we fished.

On a happier subject, I asked, "Where shall we go for lunch?"

She held my hand for a moment, then dropped it. "Before we go, I want to add a little something to your anti-suicide rant.

"Wounded, Vincent found his own way back to the Ravoux Inn by himself. True?

"There he climbed upstairs to his tiny garret room, fell into bed and asked for a doctor. That belies suicide!

"And what did he tell the police when questioned on his sick bed?"

I knew but asked. "What?"

"*Don't accuse anyone,*" he said. "A suicide certainly wouldn't say that!

"You've convinced me, Mr. Private Investigator from the sunny Caribbean. It *was* murder."

She pointed to the slack fishing lines. "Let's gather them in and go back to the hotel. Lunch there is fine with me, presuming you and Mara can restrain yourselves."

THIRTY THREE

On our way to the dining room we reminded each other about safeguarding folders and notebooks. "Your pistol still in that canvas case?"

"Absolutely," I assured her as Maurice approached our table.

"Two items for you, Mr. Kokk." He handed me a statement from the rental company and a heavy cream-colored envelope.

The first was the bill for the damaged tires replaced by the rental agency. I delayed opening the envelope since Maurice stood there expectantly.

He returned me the Renault keys. "I had them wash your car, sir. Also I gave them a copy of the police report of the vandalism," he added proudly.

I stood and shook his hand. "I'm very appreciative, Maurice. Did the police have any idea who damaged the tires?"

"Regrettably, no." He bowed slightly and disappeared into the kitchen.

Susse opened the envelope and gasped. "We are invited to lunch with Gachet at one this afternoon. Perhaps it's good news about those 'recollections.' Or..."

I finished her thought. "Lunch is supposed to soften his family's refusal to let us see those recollections. It's our farewell dinner from the Gachets."

Susse tittered, the second time since our arrival. "Shall we go for the bad news in style in our newly washed and re-tired Renault?"

Gachet met us at the door as usual and indicated seats beside a serving cart with drinks. "Welcome, welcome," he effused.

"You are very prompt despite the lateness of my invitation for which I apologize."

He wore white shirt, tie and a jacket bearing (I presumed) his family crest. Noting my look, he went into detail about the background of his family which originally came here from Normandy.

In the dining room, he continued relating family history and how the Gachets managed to survive German occupation.

"But enough of that." He raised his glass as a luncheon of vichyssoise, cheese and cold meats was served.

As the maid left, he announced "You're here to learn my family's reaction to your proposal of using our ancestor's recollections about that demented Dutch painter."

He took another sip, setting down the glass. "You may use our family Bible for your research about the van Gogh incident if you agree to our conditions. If not, no Bible."

His look turned from hospitable to hostile. "You must provide us an advance copy of the complete report made to your ministry. If we find anything objectionable about our famous ancestor--or anyone else in our family--we will take immediate legal action to halt the publication of the report. Justice must be served," he added severely, raising his eyebrows.

"Immediately our capable attorneys will petition the French government to not only object in the most strenuous manner to your government's report but take appropriate steps in retaliation."

Carefully he extracted papers from a folio. "Here are the papers you must sign, agreeing to the provisions I just outlined.

"No signature or assurances of full compliance means you don't see our family Bible containing Doctor Gachet's recollections."

I cleared my throat. "You misunderstand our purpose, Mr. Gachet. Justice is not our goal; it's 126 years too late for that. We seek only the truth."

He nodded stiffly before concluding his memorized *demarche*. "Now I'll leave you for a few minutes while you review the agreement. Please call me," he lifted a tiny brass bell from the table, "when you are ready to sign it, or depart."

More surprised by his attitude than his words, we looked at each other for a moment, then moved our chairs side by side to study the agreement.

Susse slowly translated each sentence as we sat nodding understanding at each other.

"I doubt the French government would bring legal action against foreigners like us," she whispered.

"Unless it's a criminal action." I agreed sotto voce. "It certainly could not be that."

"What shall we do? We desperately need those recollections."

I studied her concerned expression. "I think we should agree. We'll take the photographs and study them. There may be absolutely nothing in the photographs of interest."

"If there is?"

"We'll notify the embassy to come here for a copy to transmit to the Ministry. We owe them a report anyway. Meanwhile we see what's in those recollections of the revered Doctor Gachet."

"What if our Ministry objects to the agreement?"

"We return the photos to Gachet and retrieve the copy of the agreement we sign."

Susse rang the brass bell.

Once we signed the original document Gachet led us into a smaller office where an old Bible sat on an elaborate stand. Donning white linen gloves he carefully turned to the pages handwritten by Doctor Gachet.

Removing the camera from my bag, I adjusted the f-stop for lighting and snapped photos of each of the handwritten pages as Gachet slowly turned them.

He was about to close the Bible when I spoke. "May I also take a picture of the page showing the good doctor's family record?"

Anxious to see us leave, Gachet agreed and we were soon on the way back to the hotel.

"Mind if we go to the church since we're out? I'd like to ask the priest what he knows of Louis' research."

Susse agreed. "Another question, Jan, about that listening bug you found in the radio. Wouldn't there have to be a receiver nearby? Who's occupying the room next to yours?"

"Fantastic," I congratulated her. "The Schenks are next to me. Did Tania ever tell us whose gray car that is in the parking lot?"

"Here's another one." Susse grinned at the accolade. "Whose radio did you borrow? Go ask darling Mara."

"She's not speaking to me. You ask Tania. She'll know."

At the church of Auvers made famous in one of van Gogh's paintings, we parked and went inside looking for the priest. There was no one there. Outside we located the church sexton.

He paused gardening to look us over while lighting an oval cigarette. "Never heard of anyone researching our church," he claimed, pointing. "Maybe you mean the big church over there in Pontoise?"

We thanked him and returned to the hotel to call the Dutch embassy in Paris. While waiting for an embassy messenger, I wrote a summary of our activities. Explaining why we had signed Gachet's agreement was difficult. I also included the fiche of photos I'd taken of the family Bible.

Removing the radio from our worktable, we placed it in Susse's room on the farthest wall. Hopefully, this would permit us to speak more freely in my room.

"I'll not have it in my room at night," she insisted.

"Then I'll remove it before bedtime," I promised, trying not to leer.

THIRTY FOUR

That night Maurice, our host and *chef de cuisine,* prepared a marvelous *coq au vin* using fresh vegetables from his garden. Tania joined us for coffee afterwards and asked many questions about Amsterdam, which she had never visited. After satisfying her we changed the subject to our upstairs neighbors, the gray car in the parking lot and the borrowed radio.

As we uncorked a second bottle of wine the messenger from our embassy looked in from the kitchen, motioning to me.

It was Henri, who earlier had brought me the Glock pistol. Following him outside to his car, I handed him the packet I'd prepared containing my summary, the Gachet agreement and a fiche containing photos of the recollections from the Gachet family Bible.

"Please ask that these be carefully handled," I wheezed. "We need the photos back as soon as possible. The writing is hard to read so enlargements would be appreciated."

I clapped Henri Knapper on the shoulder. He jumped into the embassy sedan and left for Paris. Upstairs I found Susse at the table recording Tania's responses in her notebook.

Brimming with confidence, I placed the cognac and glasses on the table. Filling them, I offered her one.

"Only a small one, Jan. All that wine downstairs made me dizzy. I have yet another question for you, Mr. Investigator."

I raised my glass. *"Proost!"*

She leaned forward to whisper. "How do you know there aren't more snooping devices hidden in our rooms?"

"Good idea! Let's go to your room and search," I suggested in my most authoritative voice.

"Searching can be a bit tiring," I conceded. "So tiring, we might have to rest a bit before completing the entire room."

Unsteadily, she stood, hand on the door. "In your dreams, Jan Kokk! Only in your wildest dreams!"

I heard the lock on the door between our rooms snap as she left.

THIRTY FIVE

As usual there were more questions than answers to keep me awake until early morning. Chagrinned, I realized we'd made little progress in this assignment. I was being well paid by the Ministry. So well I might even consider early retirement in Curacao.

The questions persisted. Denied sleep, I dressed at six and went down to the dining room.

Several black coffees helped revive me but not enough that I understood anything but the headlines in the morning newspaper. Susse entered the room at seven, looking glamorous in fishing garb and big hat.

I held her chair. "Good morning, Susse. Ready for fishing?"

"Isn't that what you suggested last night?" Blue eyes inspected me as she sipped coffee.

Agreeing, I asked. "How were your dreams? Hook any big fish?"

She glared at me. "If I do, keep your big mitts off! I can land my own fish."

"Have that notepad with you?"

In answer, she patted her fishing vest. "Where's your canvas case?"

I lifted the case from the floor to show her. "I asked Tania to fix us a light picnic lunch rather than return here.

"I have the queasy feeling that everything we say upstairs--even here in the dining room--is being heard by someone. If not satisfied by listening, the bad guys will search our rooms.

She whispered. "Who are the 'bad guys,' Jan? Someone here in the inn?"

Unhappy that I didn't know, I hung my head. "Until we know that, we'd better do our talking outdoors."

She leaned forward to pat my hand. "Fine, Jan. That will give us more time to...."

"Fish?" I grinned.

In Paris that morning Lieutenant Fourange knocked on Captain Coffier's glass door. Inside, the captain looked up and waved him inside.

"Good morning, Captain. I have only a short report on those two Dutch nationals up in Auvers."

"Fine. Fine. Have those scoundrels looted the Louvre yet? Ha, ha."

Relieved by his captain's humor, Fourange exhaled. "They appear to be quiet up there. My informants report that their investigation seems confined to fishing in the Oise.

"The only thing reported of any significance is that person or persons unknown cut the tires on their rented car. The provincial police at Pontoise responded. No suspects."

Captain Coffier waved toward the door. "Keep me informed, Lieutenant. Let's hope they tire of fishing and leave soon."

Lieutenant Fourange saluted. "I'll get busy encouraging their departure, sir."

We sat on our customary bench once I'd baited the hooks, cast the lines and planted fishing poles in the soft earth. The weather was ideal for fishing or anything outdoors. The usual stiff winds subsided, replaced by gentle breezes. The sun shined intermittently through wispy gray clouds.

Glancing around, I saw the little gray car was absent from its usual hiding place among the trees.

Extracting pen and pad, Susse began. "I'm anxious to see those recollections of Doctor Gachet."

"Me, too. This was marvelous service on the part of our embassy. They developed and returned these photos by early morning."

She batted her eyes. "I hope you were alone when they arrived?"

"Not alone. I was enjoying my wildest dreams about you. May I describe them?"

Ignoring me, she held a page of Gachet's recollections close to her eyes. "His handwriting's terrible," she complained.

"That's a requisite for being a good doctor," I quipped, reading another page.

"Here's something," she said. "For over twenty years Gachet kept an old revolver stored on top of the armoire in his bedroom. No mention of make or caliber."

She made an entry on her pad. "That must be our missing pistol."

I countered. "Listen to Gachet's description of Vincent that Sunday."

I saw him sitting at the top of a rise in the immense field of wheat. He slumped in an old camp chair. Still folded, his easel lay beside the chair as did primed canvas atop the easel.

If I cannot paint, he said, there's no reason for me to draw a breath. He touched my hand as I turned to leave and I imagined that he had just bid me goodbye.

"The good doctor was reinforcing the rumor that Vincent shot himself in the wheat field behind the cemetery," Susse mused.

"Why would he do that?"

"His alibi! He can't be blamed for Vincent's death due to despondency which--by the way--Gachet was supposed to be treating."

"Here's more about the pistol," I squinted at the blurred handwriting in the photo.

I remembered my pistol hidden upstairs. That night I retired to my room not to rest but to load it. Breaking open the action, I loaded a cartridge into the cylinder and walked to Ravoux's house. I tiptoed into the shed where I placed the loaded revolver on the table at which Vincent usually sat. Then I returned to my home.

Susse clapped her hands. "Now we're getting somewhere!"

I cautioned. "Presuming Gachet's recollections are accurate, not fabricated. The good doctor feared he'd be accused as an accomplice."

"Or as the shooter," she made another note.

She stopped as I frowned. "What?"

"You're sure your notes are safe from prying eyes?"

She sniffed. "Under my pillow when I retire. Otherwise, here with me," she patted the vest. "Why are you so antsy?"

Searching for my pipe, I paused. "I think I must be more protective of that pillow as well as its mistress."

She punched my arm. "Seems to me Gachet's thesis, as you call it, is the opposite of mine. He's insistent the death was suicide. Agree?"

I held a match to the pipe. "I agree that he seemed to be building an alibi in case he was accused of the shooting. Wait…here's more."

The next afternoon a boy came from Ravoux's inn saying Vincent had shot himself and somehow had stumbled back to the inn. I grabbed my black bag and followed him.

I blew a smoke ring. "Suddenly Gachet was free and clear! That boy provided him an iron-clad defense!"

Susse looked up from furiously writing in her notepad. "Slow down. Is there more?"

"This is revealing, I think," I flipped through several pages about Gachet's examination of van Gogh's wound at the inn.

"Listen to this passage:

Downstairs, Ravoux was wiping off the bar and stepped from behind the counter to accompany me outside in the warm, moonlight night. 'But what I want to know, Doctor, is where did he get the gun?'

I tried to look puzzled. 'I can't imagine, Ravoux. Perhaps he brought it with him from St. Remy or somewhere in the south.'

Susse exhaled. "What a liar! If the police had located that pistol, wouldn't Gachet have been their prime suspect?"

"Exactly." I turned another page. "Here's a possible answer about the missing pistol."

I felt I had to find the gun despite the late hour. I returned to his favorite place where I had left him the previous day. I found his easel, paint box, canvas and camp stool. Searching further, I expected to find the gun in the nearby wheat…and there it was.

I wanted to erase his presence from the field. I deposited Vincent's painting equipment by the church where it would be found and brought back to the inn. The gun I intended for the river. I followed the railroad track and threw the gun into the center of a pool where the water was deep and exceedingly murky. It has never come to light.

"That's food for thought." She reached for Tania's picnic basket. "Now it's time for another kind. If we brought this food back untouched, Tania would feel badly."

I uncorked the wine bottle and unwrapped two glasses. "Here's to this new load of information!" I offered.

Susse exclaimed, "Not a load, a bonanza!"

THIRTY SIX

It was evening before we returned to the inn. Upstairs, I stared at the odd appearance of my shirt drawer. The top shirt had been moved slightly. A paperclip I'd placed under the collar was gone. Raising the bottom shirt, I found the clip beneath it.

Susse came through our common door and sat at the worktable. I turned the radio louder.

"What's wrong?"

"Someone's been here, searching my shirt drawer. Other places, too, I bet. Were your pad and notes disturbed?"

"Don't think so," she started to rise as I put the cognac on the table.

"Let's have a short one," I suggested, already half-filling the glasses.

Taking a deep breath, I spoke softly. "This means our rooms are being searched by someone who wants to know what we're finding--or writing--or both."

In soft tones Susse ticked off fingers. "The radio came from darling Mara. That gray car you're suspicious of belongs to Louis, our researcher. And..." she paused.

I couldn't resist, blurting "And what?"

"Your friend, Mara, has keys and easy access to our rooms to pry in drawers--or anywhere else."

I countered. "You left-out our next door neighbors."

"Yes, I know. That couple from Alsace-Lorraine whom we seldom see are in the room next to yours. What about them?"

I fumed. "We're nowhere in this case."

"Not true," she disagreed. "We know innkeeper Ravoux was enraged by his daughter's attraction to Vincent. That's motive."

"We know from Gachet's recollections that he felt curing Vincent's melancholy unlikely. Thinking no treatment possible, the doctor secretly provided his patient the pistol to shoot himself."

"According to Gachet," I murmured, toying with the pipe.

"There's another avenue we should explore. I hesitate to mention it because of your curious attitude."

"What attitude?" she demanded.

"Sex. We have yet to explore our painter's physical needs in Auvers. You're aware there was no brothel?"

She made a face. "That hang-up is yours, Jan. Not mine! Okay, let's discuss sex, or rather our artist's lack of it."

I sighed. "If you prefer, we can skip the subject. I know it makes you uncomfortable."

She looked wildly about the ceiling. "Think there are hidden cameras watching us in here?"

Suddenly she leaned over the table and kissed me.

I responded, surprised but very pleased with the new direction of conversation.

Sitting down, she flushed. "Don't get the wrong idea, Jan. I did that to prove my point. That 'curious attitude' as you call it is yours. Not mine!"

The next sound was the snap of her locked door as she left.

THIRTY SEVEN

"You look terrible, Jan." She greeted me the next morning at breakfast. "Didn't sleep well?"

I made a face as I sipped my coffee. "I slept very well," I lied. "Thank you."

"We're off fishing this morning? I already asked Tania to fix us another picnic lunch."

"Great," I bobbed my head hoping to fully awaken. "It's the only place we can freely...fish. I thought we might also visit the site of the shooting."

She demurred. "*If* we can find it. You know the police report mentions only the wheat field behind the church and cemetery."

"We could also check the church again to see if the priest is available."

At the church we found the priest was absent at a meeting in Pontois. We drove to the Oise and parked the Renault near our usual fishing spot.

I baited the hooks and set out poles along the bank near the bench. No gray car in sight, I noticed as we sat down.

Susse opened her notepad and began. "Let's examine the Auvers females Vincent probably saw every day. We're aware that thirteen-year old Adeline Ravoux had a schoolgirl crush on Vincent."

"True." My thoughts had been on her surprise kiss.

"He began a portrait of Adeline. For some reason she refused to sit for him a second time to finish the painting. So her portrait remains incomplete."

She parried. "The refusal may have come from her father. Perhaps Adeline complained. Her father suspected Vincent was a rascal and had designs on his young daughter.

"That daughter later told an interviewer the pistol involved in the shooting belonged to her father," I recalled. "Probably a lie."

"Never mind the pistol, Jan. Concentrate.

"The subject is sex. What other females did Vincent know or see often in Auvers?"

"Marguerite Gachet of course. She also had her portrait painted by Vincent. In fact he painted her a second time in her father's garden. There's something about her in those recollections, isn't there?"

We both searched pages of Dr. Gachet's recollections.

"Here it is," Susse announced. "Listen this from Doctor Gachet."

From time to time when I pass by Marguerite's open door, I see that a small nosegay of wildflowers has been placed on the table beneath Vincent's portrait of her. A shrine, in effect. She has not married.

Susse clapped her hands. "So Marguerite loved Vincent as did Adeline! They competed for his attention!"

"Here's another," I read from Gachet's recollections. Marguerite said:

He saw me, Papa. Monsieur Vincent really looked at me. At me.

Vincent saw something in my own daughter that I had missed. Did she imagine that she loved him, that he loved her? Had they formed a bond I failed to perceive?

She touched my collar. "I said it before, remember? That's enough motive for an angry--no, enraged--father to want to eliminate the man taking advantage of his daughter."

Susse's emotions were evident. I admired her passion. To hide it, I opened the picnic basket between us.

"Time to try Tania's picnic offering." I handed her a wrapped sandwich.

As she took the sandwich, she yelled and pointed. "Look, a fish on my line!

Slipping in her haste, Susse grabbed the fishing pole and began tugging it and walking backward. Remembering her warning about helping, I stood behind her on the slick bank.

Squealing, she alternately pulled and eased the line setting the hook on another fish.

As she began teetering on the bank, I grabbed the back of her slacks to prevent her falling into the river.

"Hands off, Kokk! This is my fight!"

Minutes later another shad lay gasping and wiggling on the grass at her feet.

"Well done!" I pounded her back.

Admiring her catch, she was oblivious. "I'm keeping this one," she panted. "I'll ask Maurice to cook it for us."

We returned to the inn where Susse entered first, triumphantly waving her fish. Maurice met us at the door wearing his usual anxious look. The last time it had been the slashed tires.

"Yes, Maurice?"

"Monsieur, the police were here. They had authorization and demanded to search your rooms."

He gestured with both hands. "What was I to do?"

THIRTY EIGHT

Susse proudly held her catch aloft. "Would you please prepare this fish for our dinner, Maurice? Meanwhile we'll go upstairs and see what damage has been done.

"Did they say why they did this?"

He took the fish from Susse, stammering. "Someone telephoned the police and reported you had drugs in your rooms."

Maurice wrung his hands. "I apologize, Monsieur and Madame. Never has this happened before. We are quiet, peaceful, honorable…"

"Yes, yes," I injected. "We know, Maurice, we know. We do not blame you for this invasion by the police."

I tried to reassure him. "Like you, we are peaceful and honorable. We are *not* drug traffickers."

Calm and unruffled, Susse asked, "Did they take anything?"

Maurice extracted a paper from his apron and offered it to her. "They took your radio for examination and left this receipt."

I touched Susse. "Let's go up and see what they've done. Then I think a dram of cognac is in order while Maurice prepares your beautiful fish."

No sooner had we started up the stairs when Susse whimpered. "Why, Jan? Why?"

She waited for me to catch up.

"An anonymous someone is harassing us by lying to the police that we have drugs. If we weren't already on a police watch list, we are now."

She frowned. "I think the bad guys want to know what direction our investigation is taking and to disrupt it.

"If it's not to their liking, they'll threaten or injure us." She hung her arm through mine as we stopped at her door.

"You go first, Jan."

Obliging, I opened wide her door.

"Oh, no!" she cried. Clothing and belongings were strewn everywhere. Her bathroom was the same, make-up and lotion bottles all over the floor.

I patted her. "I'll help you straighten up."

"Thanks but no, Jan." She took a deep breath as I opened our connecting door. "Let's see what they've done to your room before we start cleanup."

My room was a shambles. Clothing, shaving gear and personal items were everywhere beside the opened valise and suitcase. On its side but unbroken was the sturdy cognac bottle.

I tried to reassure her. "They want to frighten us away without completing the assignment."

Susse winced. "They expect us to head back to the airport first thing in the morning, maybe even tonight! But we won't run."

"Right. Let's spend a half hour putting our things away, then enjoy a drink before dinner."

Eyebrows knitted, she smiled bravely. "Better check your room again for listening devices, Jan. Maybe the police took away the old one--to find out why it wasn't working--and replaced it with a new one."

Later we sat across from each other at the worktable, toasting our adversaries. "Here's to the bad guys!" she crowed.

"May they become deaf trying to hear us above that radio."

"*Proost! M*ay they blind themselves spying on us at our fishing spot."

As we downed another drink, there was knock on the door. I opened it to find Mara staring at me in an odd manner.

"Your fish is ready," she said.

As Susse and I passed her in the hall, Mara grabbed my elbow. "I'll see you at midnight, sweetie. Leave your door unlatched."

THIRTY NINE

As we sat down at our usual table in the dining room, I felt beneath the table for wires. Watching me, Susse pursed her lips. "Find anything?"

Across the room sat the Schenks, the couple next door who seldom made an appearance downstairs. They looked up to nod, then resumed reading their newspapers.

Also in the dining room sat the other lodger, Louis Monoud who claimed to be researching the old church of Auvers. Pointedly, he waved at Susse, ignoring me.

Irritated, I forgot the question. "What did you ask?"

"Did you find anything under the table?" she repeated, pleased by my frown at Louis.

"Nothing there," I relaxed. "Maybe we can talk here as readily as when we fish. Take a look at this photo of a page from the Gachet family Bible."

Susse sipped her wine before picking up the photo. "Looks like a record of births or something."

"And deaths." I pointed to an entry. "Here's the recorded birth of Marguerite Gachet."

"So?"

"Here on the bottom of the same page is the date of her death. According to this entry, she died in March 1891."

Susse caught her breath and looked closer. "That's only months after Vincent's death.

"Strange," she frowned. "Is the cause of death given?"

"No, it wouldn't be in the family Bible, but it should be on the *arrondissement* record of her death."

Eyebrows raised, she leaned toward me. "You're thinking...."

"It's a lead," I smacked my lips, admiring the platter of fish being served us by Maurice. "We'll check it in the morning."

Mara's promptness at midnight was not as surprising as what she wore. It was a silk dressing sheath.

She stepped into my room without a word. Once inside she quietly closed and locked the door, then sat on the bed looking at me.

"We need to talk." She grabbed my arm, forcing me down beside her.

She pulled the coverlet over our heads. "You know this room is wired, don't you?"

Embarrassed and irritated, I nodded dumbly.

"The only place we can talk is under this blanket. And keep your voice low," she hissed.

I tried to sit up but Mara constrained me.

"Give me a kiss and I'll tell you what the police were after." Whispering, she pulled me back down.

"Stop it," I protested, pushing away.

Grabbing a tablet from the worktable, I handed it to her. "Here, write down what you want to say."

Surprising me, she began scribbling on the tablet. When finished, she flipped the pencil in my face.

She had written:

They were here looking for something you're writing about van Gogh and the village. Whatever it is, they left without it. They were angry. Probably will return when you don't expect it.

You owe me, Jan, and I intend to collect. Better make me happy or I'll swear to the police that you offered me drugs.

By the time I talked her out of the room it was well after midnight. I could imagine Susse listening--and suppressing laughter--on her side of the wall.

That and Mara's threat kept me awake until morning.

Adding to my embarrassment at breakfast, Mara served our table. Wearing heavy make-up, she winked each time she filled my cup.

Calling me '*Don Jan,*' Susse barely avoided laughing each time Mara passed.

"You certainly have a busy schedule," she cackled. "Sure you have time to find that records office today?"

To keep our destination from people at the inn, we stopped at a service station on the way to Pontoise for directions to the *arrondissement*.

We found the records office in less than an hour. The male registrar sitting behind a thick counter studied us as we entered. Susse fluently explained what we were looking for and he produced an immense register edged in black leather.

He sighed, put on his reading glasses, and took up a pen. "Names?" he asked.

We supplied our names, then local addresses. He looked over the rim of his glasses. "Whose record are you looking for?"

When we answered "Marguerite Gachet," he paused and studied us again. Clearly the name alerted him.

"For what purpose do you seek this record?" He removed oval glasses and polished them.

Hesitant to look at Susse, I plunged ahead with a half lie. "Mr. Gachet allowed us to study his family Bible and we are further researching it for him."

The response caused the registrar to clear his throat before beginning to carefully record my answer in another register.

"Fifty euros," he said finally, before showing us the appropriate record.

He smiled for the first time, exhibiting perfect white false teeth. "If you want a copy also, that'll be fifty euros more."

Susse and I read the ancient parchment record he offered. She nodded at me and we thanked the man and departed.

Once in the car, Susse translated the words on the death record for me. "The cause of death was abnormal bleeding caused by a breech birth," she nudged me.

In a lower tone she asked, "Did you notice the name of the attending physician?"

"Paul Gachet."

"Yes," she nodded again, touching my arm. "Her own father."

"Damn!" I beat on the steering wheel.

"What now?" Susse jumped.

"I wager Robert Gachet knows we were here--and what we looked at--within the hour.

"As Sam Spade would say '*Le chat* is out of the bag."

FORTY

On our way to the inn, I explained that Sam Spade was my favorite American fictional detective. "I admire his methods and panache."

Susse giggled. "Your idol is a fictional character? An American detective?"

Grinning, she ruffled my gray hair. "Do his methods extend to the ladies or only to murder cases?"

Pretending that parking in the inn's lot held my attention, I didn't answer. After parking and opening her car door, I confessed. "I possess none of the illustrious Sam Spade's talents, lovely Susse."

Seeing Mara seated in the dining room, Susse bussed me on the cheek as we entered. She added to Mara's annoyance by loudly whispering. "I think your talents are amazing."

We had a glass of wine as Tania prepared us another picnic lunch to take fishing. Mara sat in a corner, glaring at us until we departed. Behind Susse's back, Mara aimed her finger at me like a pistol.

"Bang!" she mouthed.

"She's beginning to give me the jitters," Susse complained. "How do you stand that old woman?"

"I don't, Susse. I attempt to keep her at arms length."

"You didn't last night," she chuckled. "Poor Jan, the women all love him, especially French fifty-year old maids."

Once at our fishing spot I baited the hooks, tossed in the lines and planted our two poles. Then I knelt down to examine the bottom of the bench.

"You're becoming paranoid, Jan," she quipped. "You see a hidden microphone behind every bush and under every rock. Did you check the picnic hamper, too?"

"Good idea." So I did. "Let's talk about this new lead on Marguerite."

Susse squirmed. "I'm hungry. Let's eat first".

Before tasting the sandwich I handed her, she turned full-face. "You have the crazy idea she was pregnant by Vincent, don't you?"

I swallowed. "I think that's a possibility."

I held up fingers as Susse had done. "One, Marguerite was his model for not one, but two paintings.

"Two, the death certificate says she died in childbirth. Three, the attending physician was her doting, avenged father."

Susse mimicked my tone. "Sounds like motive, motive, motive."

"Maybe." I opened the bottle of wine from the picnic basket. "This is all conjecture, *not* real evidence that Vincent was murdered by a vengeful father."

"Or fathers," Susse quipped.

"Don't forget Ravoux," she reminded. "He also was enraged by Vincent's interest in his thirteen-year-old daughter, Adeline. The two fathers may have decided to team together to eliminate their mutual problem."

Pouring wine into plastic cups, I studied her. "Are your notes complete enough to write a report once we're home?"

She objected. "Am I missing something? We haven't solved Vincent's death yet."

Hearing a car stopping behind us, she turned. "Uh oh. Quick, Jan! Put your pistol under those sandwich wrappers in the basket." She shoved her notepad into her bosom.

"Why?"

"The police are here. Let's hope Jan Kokk is as glib with them as he is with the engaging Mara."

I hid the pistol. On a whim, I grabbed Susse, passionately kissing her as the police walked toward the bench.

Shocked and enraged, she pushed me away and slapped me hard. "Brute!"

Bemused by the scene, two policemen stood there smirking.

I shrugged, attempting to explain in pidgin French. "The benefit was worth the blame, officers."

Grinning at either my predicament or poor grammar, one of them held out his hand.

"Fishing licenses, please."

"Clever ruse, Jan." She relented slightly after the policemen roared off in their patrol car. "Was that little act supposed to deceive me or the police?"

I poured and handed her another cup of wine. "The brute apologizes.

"No, it was certainly was not an act. I look forward to repeating it as often as you allow."

She stared at me, wondering if I was joking. She shook her head and made a face picking her notebook out of her blouse. "Luckily they didn't search the picnic basket. If they had found that pistol, you'd be on the way to jail.

"Listen to me." She poured herself more wine. "I think we must finish this business soon and get out of here while we're able.

"Is it someone at the inn who wants us to fail and leave? Or maybe it's Gachet?

I tasted the wine, wishing I'd brought the cognac. "Did Tania ever tell us whose gray car that is in the parking lot?"

"Yes, she said it belongs either to that couple, the Schenks, or to Louis."

"Strange," I frowned. "Although they live in the room next to mine, I never hear them. Poking about in the hall closet, I found a small roll of communication wire. The closet is near their door."

She entwined her fingers. "What about Louis, the church researcher? The sexton neither knows nor has heard of him. What do you make of that?"

"Too many unknowns for your humble investigator," I sighed. "As a last resort I propose we put a bit of cheese in the trap and see which rat comes after it."

She huffed. "Sounds childish to me. What exactly do you mean?"

"I'll telephone Gachet and tell him we've finished the report and that we're leaving tomorrow."

She was incredulous. "What's the cheese?"

"Your fake report."

"Where's the trap?"

"Your room."

FORTY ONE

At dinner that evening, the Schenk couple and Louis were both there as if aware we were departing the next day. "They're watching us like hawks, even listening to our banter about fishing," Susse whispered.

Eyeing Louis, Susse asked "What did Gachet say when you called him this afternoon?"

"He said he appreciated the call and hoped we had enjoyed our stay in Auvers. And…"

Her eyes brightened. "And what?"

"He hoped we had a safe trip home if we were flying Air France."

At her quizzical look, I gestured. "I'm surprised he didn't just ask for our flight number."

"Maybe he's calling Air France to present us a big bottle of champagne on departure?"

I didn't answer since Mara was pouring us coffee. On the way back to the kitchen, she slipped me a note.

Susse immediately took it from me once Mara disappeared into the kitchen.

"See you at midnight," she read aloud. "Leave your door unlocked for a treat!"

Susse tittered. "This proves you're better with the females than famous Sam Spade."

She handed me the note. "For your memoirs, *Don Jan*."

Maurice stopped by our table to ask if I wanted to clear our bill. As we started upstairs after dinner, I did so.

In Susse's room, I moved her chair into the middle of her room, facing the hallway door.

"Hey, why are you moving my furniture?"

"This is where I sit tonight waiting to see which rat comes after the cheese."

I gestured to my room. "You sleep over there. I'll be awake and alert in here."

She shook her head. "Sounds like another ruse to get me into your bed, Jan Kokk. Nothing doing! Quit dreaming!"

"Don't sleep then," I growled. "I want you over there to protect you from whichever rat comes through this door," I pointed.

"I'll be in your room waiting for your hall door to be opened by the rat. I'll have camera and pistol ready."

"If the rat fails to show, you sneak back to your room where I'm..."

I snorted. "Now you're the dreamer, Susse Thankker. Sit up all night in my room if you like. You may not stay in this room where I expect someone to break in to steal the fake report I just placed under the lamp on your night table."

Susse pointed at her hallway door. "What makes you think he or she will come through that door?"

"I told Gachet you were proof-reading the report. I'm sure everyone in Auvers knows which room you occupy."

I walked into my room and shoved the worktable in front of my hallway door, blocking entry that way.

"Keep our common door open and do not answer this one." I indicated the door I had just blocked with the worktable.

"Even if it's Mara, that aging but persistent lover?"

"Even if it's the Dutch Queen!"

"Yes, sir!" She saluted smartly. "Sir, may I have permission to use my bath before retiring to your bed?"

Ignoring her I sat down heavily in the chair I'd placed in front of her hall door. I rechecked the pistol and camera. Both were loaded and ready.

I lit my pipe, wondering which suspect would come through that door after our fake report.

Mara or Tania? Surely not Maurice!

Would the next face be that of Louis? The male Schenk? Maybe Gachet himself or a hired thug?

I checked my gold pocket watch at midnight and turned off all the lights except the lamp over the report. Exactly on time I heard knocking on the hall door in my room. From my chair I could barely hear Mara's whisper.

"Jan, darling. Open up. I want to see you so badly. Let me in."

I held my breath, hoping Susse stayed away from that door and did not reply.

The knocking became louder. Susse remained quiet. After a few minutes I heard the scratch of a key in the hallway door I sat facing.

I aimed the camera with one hand, holding the Glock pistol in the other.

Th door creeped open and a flashlight beam preceded a face exploring the room. I aimed and pressed the camera button, photographing the figure hovering in the open door.

Alarmed by the flash, the thief darted back out the door, slamming it.

The intruder was gone before I could identify him or her. I limped to the door, opened it and checked the hallway. No one was in sight.

Cursing my slowness, I turned on the lights to make certain Susse in my room was safe.

Fully dressed, she stood in our common door looking frightened. "Who was it?"

"I got a photo but not a good look. Couldn't even tell if it was a she or a he. The thief was too fast for me.

"Susse, try to get some rest while I decide the quickest way to develop this film. Hopefully it will identify our rat." Fuming, I sank back down in the chair.

"Or maybe not," she said glumly, heading back to my room.

A few minutes later the locked door in front of me burst open. While again aiming the camera at the intruder, I saw a bottle with a smoking fuse thrown on the floor.

Instantly, I snapped a photo but the flames from the shattered bottle obscured my view. Immediately the floor was covered with fire and smoke.

"Get out, Susse!" I yelled.

Grabbing a rug beneath the chair, I began beating on the burning bottle and the flames spewing out of it. The smell of gasoline filled the small room. I slammed shut the interior door between our rooms to prevent the fire from spreading toward Susse.

"Jan! Jan!" Susse screamed from the hallway. I hoped she was safe but the flames surrounding me prevented my movement.

By now Maurice and his guests stood transfixed in the hallway, most wearing pajamas or gowns. Everyone babbled while pointing at the smoke and flames.

Maurice charged toward me with an extinguisher and began spraying its contents on the spreading flames.

Confounded, he yelled. "Were you smoking in bed?"

"No, Maurice," I wiped my forehead with a grimy hand. "Someone threw a fire bomb into this room. Did you see anyone running away?"

He opened a window to dispel the smoke while I poured a pitcher of water on the smoldering rug.

Once in the crowded hallway, I pulled Susse into my room. "Are you alright? Are you alright?"

From her reaction, I was babbling, too. She gave me a reassuring hug. "I'm fine, Jan. Are you burned?"

I grabbed and held her tightly. "I was afraid you were injured."

"What now?" She looked at me oddly. "What do we do now?"

"We're leaving," I blurted. "This hotel isn't safe for us--neither is Auvers.

"We must be their next target. Since they can't steal or destroy the report, they'll be after you and I."

I replaced the pistol and camera in my canvas case. "Let's get into the car. Hopefully it wasn't torched."

"My bag," she protested.

"I loaded it last night while you were snoring in my bed.

"Goodbye, Maurice. Are all your guests accounted for?"

He wrung his hands. "You're leaving? Right now?" Maurice glanced around, counting faces.

"All but Louis," he concluded.

In fifteen minutes we were in the Renault, driving toward Compiegne and Belgium.

Susse was mystified. "Aren't we going the wrong way?"

"We're driving home, not flying. Okay?

"Finding us on the way to the airport and knocking us into a ditch would be too easy for them."

I kept peering in the rearview mirror, It looked clear: we were not being followed as we had coming to Auvers from the airport.

"I hope you won't mind a romantic trip along the peaceful River Oise. They'll be looking for us going the other way."

Susse sat closer and began wiping my face with a tissue. "Did you say 'romantic?'"

FORTY TWO

Susse read from her notepad what we'd discussed over several fishing sessions, I drove, careful not to exceed the speed limit.

To The Honorable Minister of Arts et cetera, et cetera....

"I'm skipping that part." She looked at me and I grinned in agreement.

You commissioned us to investigate the July 27, 1890 death of countryman and gifted painter Vincent van Gogh under mysterious circumstances while living in Auvers-sur-Oise, Ile-de-France.

There were several obstacles to this investigation. The incident resulting in van Gogh's death took place 126 years ago thus any remaining evidence has long been compromised. No one claimed to have witnessed his shooting. The exact location of the shooting was neither known nor reported by the police whose next day investigation was perfunctory.

"Haphazard better describes it," I fumed. "Can you imagine? There was no real investigation of a suspicious death in a quiet little village! Please continue."

The pistol used in this incident has never been recovered or fully identified as to manufacturer or caliber. The police report failed to identify the owner of the pistol involved in this shooting. During the investigation, documents were discovered which claimed the weapon belonged to the local doctor who was treating van Gogh. This document further claimed that the pistol was thrown into a deep portion of the River Oise. Another person, Adeline Ravoux, daughter of van Gogh's innkeeper, claimed the pistol belonged to her father, not the local doctor.

Susse paused. "I wonder if we're dwelling too long on that pistol?"

Slowing to study highway signs, I said, "The weapon is relevant in any shooting, especially a murder. Read more, please."

The painter lay on his deathbed at the Ravoux Inn to which he somehow had stumbled after the shooting.

The fatal bullet was not removed from his body. The location of the wound in the lower abdomen raised doubts that he could have shot himself. Entry was at an odd angle to the torso, not straightaway. Also the pistol was fired some distance from the wound, outside the normal reach of van Gogh.

No autopsy was performed by either of the attending doctors.

At the time of the incident van Gogh was receiving intermittent care and treatment from a homeopathic physician, Doctor Paul Gachet, also a resident of Auvers-sur-Oise. Doctor Gachet diagnosed his patient as suffering from melancholy and depression when van Gogh moved to Auvers in May 1890.

From rumors a local legend grew that van Gogh shot himself during an afternoon painting session at a favorite wheat field some distance northeast of the Ravoux Inn. Two witness statements refuted this. We believe the actual location was in a farmyard, behind a manure pile, about one-half mile west of the Inn.

Susse wrinkled her forehead sunburned from fishing. "Should we even mention the village rumors? It seems out of place in an investigative report."

"You're right, perceptive and lovely lady. Our report conclusions must be mostly conjecture. Most of what we have to go on is intuition plus a few scraps of evidence."

The painting implements taken by van Gogh on his outing that afternoon were never recovered. They included an easel, paint box, paints, brushes, canvases and camp stool. Their absence makes the suicide theory questionable as does the lack of a suicide note.

"You think this preamble to our findings is too long?" Susse patted my hand on the steering wheel.

"No, I think it defines our evidentiary limitations quite well." I kissed her hand.

"Let's think about where you'd like to spend the night. Or perhaps you prefer we drive all the way to Brussels today?"

Surprisingly, she placed her arm around my shoulder and squeezed. "You promised me a romantic trip along the river, not a speed trial.

"One further point," she coaxed. "You said you loaded our luggage in the car?"

"Yes?"

She pinched my ear. "While I was snoring, you claimed? I don't snore, Jan Kokk!"

"Prove it tonight." I pointed to a large hotel as we left the outskirts of Mons.

"In there," I added.

"We've yet to share a bed, literally." This sounded optimistic even to me.

She giggled. "If you keep wheedling, we never will."

I countered. "This place looks much nicer than the five-star Ravoux Inn you picked for us."

She yawned. "Pull in. I'm exhausted."

FORTY THREE

We registered in an imposing reception area, complete with crystal chandeliers. Without a murmur, argument or hysteria from her, I booked us a room with a king-size bed and jacuzzi.

I registered under the names of 'Mr. and Mrs. Henri Knapper' to avoid anyone wanting to locate and return us to France to testify in an arson investigation.

In our room I pulled the cognac bottle from my valise and, without asking, poured two large drinks.

"To you and I," I toasted. "We're still standing after eavesdroppers, tire slashers, anonymous tipsters, suspicious policemen, finally a thief and murderous arsonist.

"Did I leave anyone out?"

From the sofa, Susse raised her glass and kicked off her shoes. "You forgot that amorous maid who jumped into your bed. You also left out the person going through your shirt drawer.

"They were one and the same." I sat down beside her and began massaging her bare feet. "She didn't jump into my bed, she jumped upon it."

"If you keep parsing words," she pointed, "you'll sleep on this sofa!"

Another drink made me courageous. "I haven't heard your story, Susse. This seems like an opportune time to share."

She shrugged. "Nothing to confess. No great traumatic event has shaped my life before meeting you. No marriage, no divorce. Several good men and enough bad ones to make me swear off the male species.

"Then along came my friend Sophie, now languishing with her hateful husband somewhere on Majorca."

I leaned over her feet to kiss her. "While you languish here with a new friend in Belgium."

"You're trying too hard to be a keeper, Jan."

She surrendered another foot. "It's time I heard your sad saga. Lonely young man alone on beautiful Curacao? He decided to join the police for excitement. The excitement was lacking so he volunteered to come to the Netherlands for fun and romance?

"You must have discarded plenty of young maidens along the way to the Netherlands."

"None like you, Susse. None like you." I kissed her again.

Downstairs we had an unexpected excellent dinner of osso buco, wine, desserts and more wine.

"I thought we should begin assembling the conclusion of our investigation tonight." I began filling the oversize tub in our bath with hot water and bubbly.

"Too late for that, Jan Kokk," she tittered as I helped her into the tub. "You've spoiled me so badly I'm now putty in those big capable hands."

We put off conferring on the report.

Under a luxurious silk duvet, I was startled awake. She was softly singing in my ear.

Top of the world,
Looking down on creation,
And the only explanation I can find…

"Old song," I mumbled, turning over. She slid from my shoulder to chin.

She nuzzled me. "Old song, maybe, but I celebrate a lovely new sensation.

"You like old songs?" she peered into my half-closed eyes.

"I love that song. Who sang it?"

"Carpenters," she punched me for emphasis so I'd remember. "I'm hungry," she rubbed my neck.

"Can it wait?" I nuzzled back, rolling back to her.

Her crisp tone said my invitation to dally was denied. "It's several hours to Amsterdam, Jan. We need to finish that report, Mr. Investigator, before we get there."

Chastised, I dressed and followed her to the dining room for breakfast and to check out. Within the hour we were back on the road to Brussels.

"Sleep well?"

"You expect a 'well-done' for your nocturnal mischief, don't you?" Susse bit my ear.

"Your verdict?"

"Passable," she conceded. This time she kissed the tingling ear.

Settling back in the passenger seat she pulled out the notepad. "Let's get started on that report. Facts first."

"We have very few of those," I reminded.

"Then start with probable motives."

Avoiding a sneeze, I began. "Father number one was Doctor Gachet. His motive is the stronger of the two, I think. His daughter was enthralled, then intimate, with his peculiar on-again, off-again mental patient."

"She allowed Vincent to paint her in two poses." Susse made rapid notes. "Once playing the piano and again, standing in the Gachet garden."

"Marguerite and Vincent enjoyed an intense personal relationship." I began.

"We deduce this since her father was enraged at Vinc…"

"As he should have been," she broke in. "Vincent impregnated his daughter. Who else could it have been?"

My turn. "Her doting father attended her during pregnancy and an abnormal delivery during which she died.

"What gossip that must have provided Auvers' villagers. No wonder the current Gachets are so defensive and reticent.

"Father number two," she held up her pen, "also had a motive. His daughter Adeline, all of thirteen years, also was enamored--is that the word--with thirty-seven year old Vincent, the upstairs lodger in her father's inn."

Susse hesitated. "Should we say lodger or guest?"

I slowed to read more highway signs. "Seems to me lodger is more accurate."

"D'accord. Lodger, it is."

I couldn't stop. "Innkeeper Ravoux was suspicious and apprehensive--no, highly angered--by the attention given his daughter by this foreign lodger. Adding to Ravoux's displeasure was that his tenant often was unable to settle his room bill of 150 francs a month."

"Adeline may have been frightened of the Dutch lodger," Susse suggested.

"Why frightened? You said she was enamored."

Susse admired a windmill in the next field as we passed. "Remember? She refused to sit a second time for Vincent to finish her portrait. Vincent painted Marguerite twice, once at the piano and again in the garden."

"Although only thirteen, Adeline realized Marguerite, her competitor, was gaining."

"Further supposition?"

I blinked from the sudden bright sun, then donned sunglasses. "The two fathers, Gachet and Ravoux, were long-time friends. Sharing a serious mutual problem, they decided to work together to solve that problem."

She nodded. "Make Vincent leave Camelot or..."

"Eliminate him," I finished the thought. "What about that troublesome pistol?"

With a shake of her head, she answered. "Gachet claimed it was his. He said he recovered it after the shooting and threw it into the deepest, darkest pool in the river."

"But Adeline," she turned a page, "claimed during a later interview that the pistol belonged to her father. All the police reported was that the weapon was never found.

"She changed her story several times over the years. Adeline wanted her father to become as famous as his lodger, her dream lover."

Rubbing my forehead, I turned. "Want to stop in Brussels?"

Susse seemed determined. "No, let's keep going. We could spend tonight somewhere in the Netherlands nearer home."

"D'accord," I surprised her with my improved accent. She batted her eyes at the feat.

FORTY FOUR

"Now we explain our theory how the two fathers executed their plan," I began.

Susse demurred. "Say 'implemented' instead of 'executed.'"

"Implemented, it is" I concurred. "Gachet provided the means, his pistol. Ravoux supplied the intelligence, where van Gogh had gone to paint that Sunday afternoon."

Susse partially rolled down a side window. "Two witnesses saw Vincent leave the inn and walk westward where he entered a farmyard on Rue Boucher."

"The fathers followed Vincent into the farmyard, found him behind a big, concealing manure pile, and…" I paused to let her finish.

She complied. "The two fathers confronted Vincent. An angry argument flared and the determined fathers completed their plan, shooting Vincent but in the lower abdomen."

"Which father fired the shot?"

"Doesn't matter," she shook her head. "Both were guilty. They picked up his painting gear, stool and pistol and disposed of that evidence on the way back to their homes."

"Rehearsing their supporting alibis all the way back."

I probed. "Why leave Vincent only wounded?"

"They thought the wound was fatal. He would die there unable to move or speak."

We slowed, nearing the Dutch border. Susse sat up as we stopped to show passports to the frontier officers.

I tested her theory. "Vincent knew who shot him. Why would he later insist to the police 'Accuse no one?'"

She checked her hair in the mirror. "Acute depression. The fathers' accusations rang the death knell in his fragile mind. He had impregnated a daughter. He had no money to care for her, a child or himself, much less continue to meet his meager expenses.

"His painting didn't sell. He couldn't even pay for the paint and canvases he had just ordered without begging brother Theo to again bail him out.

"Doctor Gachet hated his patient for what he'd done to Marguerite. Oddly enough, the patient still regarded Gachet as a friend and fellow-sufferer."

Susse grabbed my hand on the steering wheel. "Can you imagine the effect this enormous load of guilt had on already despondent Vincent?"

"Somehow he imagined his shooting was providential. He welcomed death?"

"Yes, Jan. He welcomed death."

Instead of relief that we had outlined the substance of our report, we were depressed by its telling. Ahead was a service station and restaurant so I pulled over to gas up the car.

"I'll get us a table and order coffee." She headed for the restrooms. I filled the fuel tank, locked the car and followed her inside.

She'd chosen a small formica table with paper napkins and the kind of uncomfortable wire chairs found in old soda fountains.

A waitress appeared as I sat opposite Susse. "Coffee?" she asked, handing us menus. We looked at each other for confirmation and nodded.

"What's good today?" Susse asked.

"The leek soup but it's almost gone."

I took Susse's wink as my cue. "Two leek soups to begin, please."

Susse grinned as she saw my hand searching the underside of the table. "Find any wires? Are the bad guys still tracking us?

Her tone dropped an octave. "Speaking of the bad guys, who were they, Jan? Why did they try to frighten and harm us?"

"You're dazzling this morning," I said, trying to assemble a good answer.

Ignoring me, she answered herself. "The only absentee from those people in the hall after the fire was Louis. He must have been the one who tried to steal the fake report from my bed table.

"When he failed that because you surprised him with the camera, he threw a bottle of gasoline at you to destroy the report. You, too!"

Despite the brief time we'd known each other, I'd been amazed that we often read each other's thoughts.

"As I said in Amsterdam, you'll be a superb investigator on our team."

She frowned at 'our team' but continued. "Who is Louis really and why did he try to harm us?"

Blowing on the hot coffee, I began. "When the sexton at the church didn't know anything about Louis, I asked the embassy's security officer to check him out."

"And?"

Susse erupted, another example of our identical thinking. "Louis' last name is Gachet!"

"Not..." She'd forgotten Louis' last name.

"Monoud," I helped. "He registered at the inn as Louis Monoud but he's a Gachet, placed in the inn to keep tabs on us."

"Also to derail us if we discovered--and tried to report--the true story about Vincent's shooting?"

Grinning, I admired her as more coffee was served. "Soup's coming," the waitress said on her way back to the kitchen.

Susse tasted the coffee and winced. "Strong stuff. You mean your stalker, Mara, was completely innocent?"

She arched an eyebrow. "Wasn't it Mara who searched your shirt drawer."

Still cooling my coffee, I agreed. "I suppose she was just curious about us."

She chortled. "Not us. You, handsome Caribbean man."

Arrival of the soup diverted us until we'd finished it. Placing a napkin in her lap, she squinted at me.

"So it was Louis who made the anonymous telephone call to the police that caused them to search our car and rooms?"

I nodded, reading the menu. "Now let's order something more substantial. How about the veal?"

"Not at a roadside restaurant, Jan. How about a nice omelet?"

150

"Suits me." I looked around for a public telephone. "Don't you know the art editor at the *Amsterdam Telegraff*?"

"Sure. Nelle is a close friend. We were at the university together. Why?"

"We need to leak the story about the fire at the Ravoux Inn, including the 'who' and 'why.' That ought to keep the Gachet family too busy to notice, then deny our report."

FORTY FIVE

VAN GOGH HOME IN AUVERS TORCHED
SUSPECT QUESTIONED BY POLICE

Paris- Reuters News

Paris Police confirmed last night that the former Auvers-sur-Oise hostel of famous Dutch painter Vincent van Gogh was burglarized and fire-bombed Tuesday.

A suspect, as yet unnamed by Police but believed to be a member of a prominent Auvers family, was being held for questioning.

According to unofficial sources, the suspect attempted to burglarize a room of the famous Ravoux Inn where van Gogh boarded prior to his death in July 1890.

Unable to complete the planned burglary, the suspect threw an incendiary device into the room. The resulting fire, eventually extinguished by alert occupants, caused no injuries but damages estimated at Euros 30,000.

At press time, possible motives for the attempted theft and completed arson are unknown. Auvers mayor Jean-Claude Vallet made the following statement to this reporter last night.

"We are shocked and appalled by this criminal activity in our peaceful village where van Gogh's memory and art are revered. We hope the guilty party or parties are soon charged and prosecuted to the full extent of the law."

Susse hooted while handing me the newspaper article we'd picked up in the vestibule of our Amsterdam hotel. "Nelle's article is a great prelude to the Ministry's announcement of our report.

"She told me her story has already been picked up by Rotterdam, The Hague and, of course, *Paris Match*, complete with a photo of the inn."

While pouring us a congratulatory cognac I succeeded in kissing her neck.

On arrival in Amsterdam, she urged me to move into her apartment but I hesitated, thinking of the publicity Nelle's article would generate.

Our investigation report would eventually be publicized and Susse's involvement made public. I wanted to minimize her hounding by the press.

Practical as always, Susse tapped the keyboard in her lap holding her empty cognac glass. "We've got to finish this report and turn it in at the Ministry, Jan.

"No fooling," she shook her head at my offer of another cognac. "Let's start the finale of the report. I'm expected to return to work at the museum soon.

"Unless…" she began, giving me the eye.

Our thoughts coincided: I knew exactly what she meant. To delay an answer I began dictating a draft conclusion to our investigation. She began copying it on the keyboard.

In the absence of facts over the 126 year old period since van Gogh's death, the following are the conclusions of the investigators.

First. Absent a witness, suicide note, the pistol used in the shooting, an autopsy of the deceased, or a comprehensive police report, it is concluded that van Gogh was shot by person or persons. He did not commit suicide, contrary to popular legend.

Second. Van Gogh was a lonely man searching for companionship in the small village of Auvers. He discovered it in the persons of two young females. One, thirteen-year old Adeline Ravoux, was the daughter of the innkeeper from whom van Gogh rented a room. The other female, Marguerite Gachet, aged nineteen, was the daughter of the local physician who occasionally treated van Gogh for melancholy and depression.

Third. Both the Ravoux and Gachet fathers were highly angered by the attentions paid by their daughters to van Gogh and vice-versa. Both suspected van Gogh's relationships with their daughters were more than platonic. Marguerite Gachet, the model for two if his paintings, may have become pregnant by van Gogh.

Rage at van Gogh—-thus motive--was shared by both fathers. Eventually, they collaborated to force his departure from Auvers and their daughters.

The opportunity to exercise their plan came on Sunday, 27, 1890. Van Gogh left his lodging to paint in a nearby farmyard. The fathers followed, armed with a pistol belonging to one father. They confronted van Gogh in the farmyard about his relationships with their daughters. The argument must have turned angry and one of the enraged fathers shot van Gogh in the lower abdomen.

There is no indication or evidence about which of the fathers fired the eventually fatal shot. Could the shooting have been an accident? We cannot answer.

In conclusion the investigators wish to inform you that publication of this report may draw criticism, possibly retaliation, from the Government of France, where van Gogh's death was conveniently labeled a suicide.

(signed):

Jan Kokk Susse Thankker

As she read the last portion, Susse drew her breath. "You want me to sign this report as if I'm a real investigator?"

I succeeded in filling her empty glass. "Didn't we agreed that we are a team?"

"Then let's practice a little team work," her eyes sparkled. "First, in the shower…"

FORTY SIX

The next morning my attempt at singing awakened her.

Love, look at the two of us
Strangers in many ways...

"Why, Jan! You have a great voice. You should sing more often."

"You inspire me! Know that song? It's also by the Carpenters."

Her happy mood disappeared once we went downstairs. Staring out the dining room window at bustling Amsterdam, she whispered. "I must call Sophie."

"I know," I nodded, reading her thoughts. "Why not make your call from our room, I'll be in the bar. Call me when you're through."

The shaved-head burly bartender and I traded military stories--some true, some not--while I had a beer. One beer became two, then three as I waited for her call.

Knowing she had gone without saying goodbye, I trudged upstairs, hoping for a note.

I scoured our room. No note. All her things were gone.

Instead she had printed our report to the Ministry. I sat on the bed where I found it. After reading it through, I signed my name beside hers.

The case was closed. My assignment completed except to deliver the report to the Ministry, which I could accomplish on my way to the airport.

What now? The sudden finality of closure--of both the report and our relationship--darkened my mood.

Back downstairs at reception, I dashed off a terse cable to Robert Gachet in Auvers.

"Your family's criminal act at the Ravoux Inn abrogates our written agreement. No advance copy of my report will be furnished you. Kokk."

Not wanting to spend the evening in the bar, I packed, then repacked my valise and suitcase. The cognac was almost gone, but it aided my sleep.

That night there was no news from Susse. I expected none.

After breakfast the next morning, I visited the travel office next door and made arrangements for my flight home to Willemstad.

Stopping by the van Gogh Museum I hoped to see Susse but--no surprise--she was not there. Probably with Sophie, I imagined.

Everything seemed too sudden, too final. Shaking my head, I flagged-down a van heading to Schiphol airport. At the airport gift shops, I filled my pockets with small bottles of cognac for the long flight to Curacao.

On board the luxurious KLM airbus to Barbados, then Willemstad, I selected an aisle seat near the rear of the aircraft. That's where the younger, lovelier attendants are assigned.

"Lovelier," I examined the word aloud. "Derivative of 'love.' How did that work out on this trip?" I asked.

"Your name, sir?"

An attractive young female attendant stood beside me, clipboard in hand.

Bollixed. I imagined I was seated at my desk in Willemstad trying to pay monthly bills.

Dazed, I replied in Papamientu. "Bon dia."

Grinning at my confusion, she blinked. "From that accent, you must be Mr. Jan Kokk from Curacao. We have a radio message for you from Amsterdam."

"Thank you," I managed. Noting her trim figure, smile and dark eyes, I make a guess.

"You from the Antilles?"

She smiled, eyes twinkling. "Good deduction, Mr. Kokk. But your line is just mediocre."

"I'm Jan," I attempted another. "And I hope to learn more about..."

"Anita, Jan. I'm from Bonaire. There's a long flight ahead of us so I'm sure you'll have plenty of time to ask me questions."

With that she turned and wiggled forward to the galley. Halfway there, she spun around and waved.

I crumpled the Amsterdam message and put it in the seat pocket.

Printed in the United States
By Bookmasters